S0-BBD-943

The Masters Review

ten stories

The Masters Review

The Masters Review Volume VII
Stories Selected by Rebecca Makkai
Edited by Sadye Teiser and Cole Meyer

Front cover:
Design by Kim Winternheimer

Interior design by Kim Winternheimer

First printing.

ISBN: 978-0-9853407-6-6

© 2018 *The Masters Review*. Published annually by *The Masters Review*. All rights reserved. No part of this publication may be reproduced or reprinted without prior written permission of *The Masters Review*. To contact an author regarding rights and reprint permissions please contact *The Masters Review*. www.mastersreview.com

Printed in the USA

The Masters Review

ten stories

Volume VII

Emma Sloley • Rebekah Bergman

Andrea Uptmor • Jeanne Panfely • Robert Glick

Blair Lee • Carrie Grinstead • Rebecca Gummere

Anna Reeser • Laura Demers

Stories Selected by Rebecca Makkai
Edited by Sadye Teiser and Cole Meyer

Contents

Introduction

What does it mean to be an emerging writer? All I know is that I was labeled as such at one point—I was invited to several festivals featuring "emerging writers," all around the time when I had stories out but no novel, or one novel and no clue what was supposed to happen next—and that sometime thereafter, with no warning, I stopped emerging. It felt wildly unfair to me at the time, because wasn't I just a brand-new little baby writer with nothing but exciting promise? But no: By the time your second book appears, apparently you've emerged. Recently, I was joking with a couple of friends (writers who "emerged" before I did, and more thoroughly than I ever have) about launching, for those of us who've been around the block, a Submerging Writers Festival.

Which is all to say: I know, I remember, that this "emerging" thing is both fun and terrifying. As much as I look back with nostalgic longing at the moment when my first story was accepted for publication—when everything was potential and excitement—it's only now from this point, looking back, that I know what that moment was the start of. At the time, for all I knew, it was a fluke. It was a mistake, soon to be corrected with an awkward follow-up note. The journal would fold before the story came out. A printing error would omit half the piece. No one would even read it. Everyone would read it, in horror that it had been published.

When the journal in question finally arrived at my house (nine whole anguishing months later!) I couldn't bear to look directly at the story. I made my husband look at it and check that it was real, that all the words were there, that they'd spelled my name correctly.

To judge any contest is daunting, but one for emerging writers is especially so. There's the question, first of all, of what this would mean to the writers chosen—something I have no way of knowing. Is this a writer on the verge of giving up, or one who's received ten acceptances and a six-figure book deal this year? If I squint hard enough, can I tell? (No; I cannot.) And then there's the question of promise versus polish. Everyone here has an abundance of both, but for the final spot, as I'm considering a story weighted more towards spark and promise against one weighted more towards polish. . . . Which way do I go? (Well: spark and promise. But not without a lot of hair-pulling.)

What I'm always looking for, in everything I read, is the airplane factor. I don't mean whether or not I'd enjoy this on an airplane. I mean: *Is this a good pilot?* Does this pilot stall out on the runway, or are we up in the air before I know it, happily captive to the plane's course? Do we fly along smoothly enough that I can take in the world from this height, see new things, or am I jolted along, constantly reminded that I'm in an airborne tin can? And finally— and, good lord, this is the hardest thing—can this pilot land the plane? I've had so many wonderful reading flights (award-winning books included) end with an unceremonious *thunk*. A great ending shouldn't just conclude a story but add to it. I'll go further: A story is largely just a vehicle to get to the ending. The ending should be the whole point. Just like landing safely at O'Hare is the whole point, no matter how much you enjoyed your flight.

One story here, "Little Room," could be its own master class in endings. I loved it all along, and had no clue where it was going, and when it ended with a lovely gut-punch from the side, it leapt straight into my *yes* pile. Another story, "The Sand Nests," made me cheat and peek at the ending before I was done. It was partly because the plot had me in such a state of panic that I needed to know how things would turn out; and partly because I loved it so much that I needed to know, right then and there, that the author had not muddled the ending. (In fact, she absolutely nailed it.)

Some stories I found so wildly entertaining that I forgot I was flying above the earth and managed just to enjoy a view I'd never experienced. "Rogue Particles" was like that, its core a broken friendship so compelling that I read the story in one huge gulp. "Shrove Tuesday" is so strange and liquid that it swept me up with its first line and just kept going. "The Collectors of Anguish" had me worried for its characters from the very start, and wouldn't let me look away.

And once in a while there's a story that keeps you constantly in mind of its form. (I've never flown in a hot air balloon, but for the sake of keeping this strained metaphor going, I'll say that when you're in a hot air balloon, you never forget it, but that's kind of the point.) "Questions for Anesthesiologists" and "Pilgrimage" both play with form to great effect, drawing attention to their own structure in ways that enhance rather than detract from the message. The snapshot narration of "The Process" kept me riveted not just to the story but to the angle of its telling.

Other stories took me places I wasn't expecting, and I'm always thrilled when I can't tell from the first paragraphs what a story is going to be about or where it will land. "Ghost Print" and "Doctor, Doctor, Doctor" did that for me—and not just because the courses of the stories kept changing, but because the point-of-view characters kept changing in fundamental ways as well.

What I can say, at the end of it all, is that these writers are truly and fully emerging. Their work is ready for you, if you're ready for it. These are voices you'll be hearing from quite a lot, voices with some lungs behind them. If you happen upon this anthology years from now, you might smile at the notion that some of these writers were ever considered new.

To the ten writers chosen, and indeed to all thirty of the writers whose work I was privileged to read and to consider: Yes, this is it. Big things are happening, because you're ready, and the world is a dumpster fire but we need you and we need your stories to take us up above it all. This is it. Ready for liftoff. Let's go.

—*Rebecca Makkai*

The Masters Review

ten stories

The Sand Nests

Emma Sloley

Only two days have passed since they were banished to the boat but already the summer's inevitable fractiousness has made itself apparent. They know there is always this period of adjustment, this is their sixth year now under this arrangement, but it doesn't get easier, shrinking their lives to fit the space. The wife, Caroline, especially hates the futility of spending hours hunting for some object that would have had its own, immutable place in their usual home. Her husband Paul curses every time he smacks his head on a low doorway, which on a boat is every doorway. The only one happy is Everett, who at nine years old still possesses the ability to be enchanted.

For her sake they try to think of it as an adventure as well, but out of the child's earshot they default to grousing about the conditions: the stifling heat; the difficulties of cooking and sleeping; the haunting reek below decks; the temerity of their greedy landlord, who temporarily evicts them every time high season comes around so she can rent out their cottage for a sum so enormous as to carry a whiff of the obscene. They happily pay the obscenity though, the summer people, so Paul and Caroline and Everett are required to clear out every June and decamp to this repurposed lobster boat moored in the old, unfashionable marina at the windswept northern tip of the peninsula. The other marina, the fancy one, is situated halfway up the coast, and bristles with superyachts and people who care about shoes.

Caroline had driven to the fishermen's dock earlier and bought two small perch wrapped in waxy paper. She bastes the fish in olive oil, lemon, salt, and oregano and lays them on the grill of the tiny barbecue on the aft deck. They both loathe cooking in the poky galley downstairs, so most meals are prepared, cooked, and eaten on deck, unless the weather turns bad. Which it often does in these parts, dumping summer squalls that feel specifically engineered by some cruel unseen hand to fray their relationship. Paul takes several trips to bring the salad ingredients up the stairs, cradling Tupperware containers in the crook of one arm while he holds the rail with the other. The marina is sheltered but even so a strong wave under the hull can pitch a person off-balance hard enough to sustain a nasty bruise.

Everett sits cross-legged inside a coil of thick rope, playing a game on her ancient phone. She glances up when Caroline calls her to set the table. From this position her mother is merely a set of legs, slender and threaded with varicose veins. Caroline feels swollen a lot these days, a bloated fish washed ashore, but to Everett the veins are beautiful, the delicate color of lavender. She has assigned this color the number fifteen, or rather it has been assigned for her, and she whispers the number now. "Fifteen."

Paul overhears but they are both used to the girl pronouncing numbers out of nowhere. Other issues prick at his equilibrium with greater urgency. He comes to stand beside Caroline, depositing the containers on a plastic table once white but now scarred and jaundiced from the elements, and begins to chop the ingredients and toss them into a wooden salad bowl he thinks he remembers receiving as a wedding gift. They leave all their glass and ceramic possessions locked up in a special closet in the cottage over the summer, bringing with them only tin and wood and plastic and iron, the depressing unbreakables. As he tosses the salad he turns toward her to share the thought that had been marinating all day.

"Have you noticed how everyone we know is overeducated and underemployed?"

"Hmmm?" Caroline says, although she heard him fine and is simply employing a reflexive stalling tactic. "Including us, I suppose you mean."

"Oh sure. It's kind of weird though, isn't it? We used to all be so busy. Now everyone is always free for lunch, but no one can afford to go out to eat."

She sighs, turns the fish over. There is a miniscule bolt of simple joy at seeing how beautifully the flesh has taken on the black grill marks. But why does he have to give voice to such things? The trick to tolerating lies is forgetting. If you're always harking back to some golden age of gainful employment and ambition and easy friendships, back in the hazy years before children and the financial crisis, then how will you keep your balance in the present? Some of their old friends have drifted back to the Midwest, or the West Coast. Some have taken jobs in marketing or precarious tech-adjacent industries. Some, like the two of them, decided to slip away from big-city life altogether.

"Not like we see any of them except in the off-season, anyway," says Caroline in her proud, wounded voice, because now that he has started on the topic she is glad to pick away at the scab.

A lot of the friends whose lives have become impoverished take any opportunity to visit during the fall, winter, and part of the spring, when Caroline and Paul have possession of the cottage. "If only you had this place year-round!" they cry, like plaintive seagulls. The friends roll up with children and exotic cheeses and fisherman sweaters and sometimes picnic baskets in case the weather behaves. There are games and too much wine and endless wood-fires, which sound so romantic unless you're the person tasked with chopping the wood. No one comes to visit in the summer. It makes sense—where would they sleep if they did . . . on the boat's deck?—but there is still a sting in this blatant signaling of what the friends value.

"They're like the opposite of fair-weather friends," Paul says.

"Foul-weather friends."

"Exactly."

Paul covers the salad with a dish cloth to keep the flies away, then opens a bottle of sauvignon blanc and stands holding the plastic flute by the base while he surveys the bounds of their seasonal world: the scattering of embattled fishing boats and humble pleasure cruisers bobbing in the oil-slicked water, a stubby pier with a rusted fuel pump, a boarded-up tackle store and four ugly bulbous green recycling bins on shore. (Everett could have told him that this particular shade of green corresponds to the number four.)

"Why do you keep touching yourself down there?"

He is startled out of his thoughtless reverie by Caroline's sharp voice. He turns to face her. She is holding the tongs aloft like a weapon or a trophy, cheeks flushed from the heat of the grill, her lips slightly parted, strands of her dark-blond hair floating around her face. In another era he might have playfully tackled her for the tongs, tickled her, or at least smoothed the strands behind her ear, hoping it would lead to hijinks. In this era his hand still goes to his groin, but only to worry at the lump that had appeared there, when? A few weeks ago . . . a couple of months? He panics at how quickly he has lost track.

"I'm sure it's nothing, Caro. But do you mind coming and feeling it?"

He stands there with his shorts pushed down around his hipbones, feeling vulnerable and ludicrous while she frowns and gingerly rubs her fingers over the spot. There is something proctological about it, even though it's not that side of the body, something to do with the feeling of helpless diminishment that comes from standing in a paper gown in a doctor's office waiting to be probed. When she raises her chin, her eyes meet his and he sees the fear he has been pushing down written there. Caroline swivels, using her back to screen their conversation in case Everett is watching, which seems unlikely, given how monumentally boring she finds their company.

"I'm going to call Dr. Kim. Make an appointment."

He begins to demur but after all this is what he had wanted—for someone else to take responsibility for the situation. If she takes it in hand then everything that follows will be her responsibility too. He banishes this thought as unworthy of the decent person he still aspires to be.

Caro being Caro, she instructs Paul to continue supervising cooking of the fish and the sliced fried potatoes while she makes the call right away. He doesn't know whether he hopes for an appointment immediately or at some undesignated time far in the future. But he sees from her relieved face when she comes back from the wheelhouse—where the cell signal is strongest—that it is the former.

"He can fit us in on Thursday," she says. "Thank god."

"That's good," he says, feeling a little faint. The lump, which even this morning occupied no more than a tiny closet of his mind, has now moved in and taken over the entire space, every nook and cranny poisoned with worry.

There is no thought of taking Everett with them. She has a horror of doctors. Just imagining performing the additional emotional labor of keeping her calm is exhausting. Now that the decision has been made a deadening feeling of inevitability overcomes them both, and they eat dinner on the deck sunk in silence. The sky shifts from yellow to purple to deep blue to black, and Everett converts each of them in her head: fifty-two, fifteen again, forty-eight, nineteen, and three. The air gets chilly out in the open once the sun has gone down. It's too early in the season yet for the true balmy nights, but they pull blankets out of a trunk, shake them out and wrap themselves up, three little cocooned souls adrift in exile. The muffled beat of electronic music drifts across the sand dunes from a party somewhere down the coast.

*   *   *

Thursday both takes forever and arrives far too quickly. Only a few days have elapsed, yet they have both become amped to the edge of hysteria by the prospect that the lump might turn out to be Something Bad. Now that it has been spoken of, it belongs in the world as much as they do. He lies awake wondering what Caro and Everett will do without him. She lies awake wondering the same thing. The unthinkable is suddenly all they can think about.

She is solicitous of him now, tiptoeing around their conversations as though his feelings are a church. This is the one silver lining, that they have rediscovered kindness in one another. They have stopped squabbling altogether. They both hug Everett for a few extra seconds every night before bed. She is an intuitive child but she seems not to notice anything amiss, and they congratulate themselves on successfully shielding her from the horror of this gnawing worry, when really they have just willfully misdiagnosed her intuition—she is uncommonly attuned to the natural world and the world of objects, but at this age other humans lie outside her realm of interests.

They both rise early and Caroline cooks scrambled eggs, willing to face even the galley to simulate an atmosphere of normality. Nothing feels normal though. Paul knows something has changed because when he passes the kitchen he sees that she has left the pots to soak rather than cleaning them right away. The rule is that whoever cooks cleans up also, to give the other person a whole meal off, but often when it's her turn she claims the dishes are extra-encrusted and need to soak overnight, knowing full well he can't stand squalor and will end up doing them. This subversive laziness usually infuriates him but today the sight doesn't register at all on the rancor scale. This, more than anything else, scares him.

By silent consensus they seem to have decided not to tell their daughter about the Something Bad. Why spoil her week, too?

"What are your plans today, Everett?" Paul asks, ruffling her cotton-candy fine hair.

"Going to look for mussels," she answers without hesitation. Paul has shown her how to scrape them off the rocks with a sharp stone or a small knife.

"Not without Daddy though. Let's do that later on. Maybe tomorrow."

She pouts for a second, on the verge of protesting, then she seems to forget all about it in favor of running one of her rope-soled sandals around the railings as if along a monorail, her face alight with concentration.

Sometimes he envies the child her easy joy. She enters each new situation with an expectation of pleasure, and this innocent entitlement is often rewarded. He can scarcely believe how wide the gulf is between the part of his life when he knew such pleasure and the time he is currently inhabiting, one in which his most decadent habit has become crying in his used Toyota Corolla in the sparsely populated lot adjacent to the marina. He spends two days a week working as an adjunct professor at the third-rate liberal arts college that is a two hours' drive away, and those twenty hours a week are so thoroughly demoralizing that he sometimes barely makes it off campus before his throat tightens. If there is one life lesson he feels he could impart to his students, those barely adults still starry-eyed and fattened on idealism, it would be that there's nothing noble about having money, and nothing sexy or romantic about not having money. Not that he would have listened to him at their age.

After breakfast there are still five terrible long hours to pass until they can leave for the appointment. They let Everett loose as soon as everything is cleaned up, as is the usual routine during these warm months. She skips down the pier, waving spastically over her shoulder in their direction, her backpack bumping against her bony legs as she runs toward the sand dunes. They've made sure she's a strong swimmer, is perpetually slathered with sunscreen, and always has plenty of water and her phone charged when she leaves the house, so there's no reason Paul should feel this unfamiliar anxiety that clutches at his chest as he watches her disappear into the shimmering landscape. Every emotion is just super-charged since they dragged the Something Bad into the light.

"Hey Caro?"

"What?"

"Meant to tell you. You know Cal, the old dude who lives down in the fishing shack?"

He's not sure why he calls him old, when the guy is probably only ten years older than they are. An Iraq War veteran whom some of the local year-rounders have been trying to get evicted by claiming he lives there illegally, squatting, though no one really knows this for sure. There's no septic and he lets his trash pile up at the back of the shack. It's unsanitary, they say, it attracts rodents and god knows what else. Other offenses: he smokes a noxious smelling pipe and has a tendency to go on profanity-laced rants whenever strangers approach the shack.

Caroline emerges from the head, drying her hands on a towel. "What about him?"

"Josh told me that someone saw him the other day sitting outside his place, squatting on the sand untangling a fishing net or something. Buck naked."

They both take a moment to conjure up this unwelcome vision; the saggy tattooed flesh, a thatch of graying chest hairs, the pendulous scrotum dangling between his ankles. She realizes the story is supposed to be comical or to evoke outrage, but her first reaction is to come to Cal's defense, although she barely knows him.

"I get that he's kind of weird, but that doesn't mean he deserves to get kicked out."

"Oh, I agree, he's harmless. Just thought it was funny, him being a nudist. He once gave Everett a little wooden box covered with shells, remember?"

"How could I forget? She covets that thing."

Despite their shared distaste for the local torch mob's enthusiasm to evict the poor man, they have suggested to their daughter that it might be a good idea not to visit with Cal unless they accompany her. Naturally she couldn't just accept this edict but demanded to know why. "Just because." As far as they know, she has obeyed.

When they're fifteen minutes away from leaving for the appointment, Caroline phones Everett.

"Where are you, honey?"

"Visiting the sadness."

"What?"

"I said visiting the sand nests. Where the little birds lay their eggs. Waiting to see if any hatch."

"Oh, OK. Well, Paul and I are driving into town to see the doctor. We'll be home in time to make dinner. Will you be all right?"

"Yeah."

"Don't stay out too late. Go back to the boat before it gets dark."

"OK."

Is it strange that the girl didn't ask why they were going to the doctor? Is that another item to add to the worry to-do list? She can't think about it right now. Her heart is hammering so loudly she fears he will hear it, quickly turns the volume on the radio up with clammy fingers. Paul is looking out the window, face closed, his bottom teeth jutting out. She would have preferred to talk, to paper over the nervousness with chatter, but every conversation she attempts turns into a cul-de-sac. He just nods or gives a monosyllabic answer, and she soon gives up so they can sink into their separate miseries.

*   *   *

The doctor's office is like all such places: simultaneously suffused with an end-of-the-world surrealism and the all-too-real banality of sickness.

"Paul Balamo?"

Paul stands abruptly, a racehorse eager to get out of his constricting gate, but Caroline rises more awkwardly. One leg seems to have become tangled beneath her. "Sorry," she murmurs to nobody. She squeezes his hand and they move wordlessly towards the doctor's room. The door is ajar and they can see the doctor at his desk, sipping from a can of Diet Coke. She closes the door behind her, because whatever happens now is just between the three of them, as in some secret lovers' pact.

*   *   *

They walk back out to the car without speaking. It feels to her as though they haven't spoken for days, that this entire expedited crisis has unfolded in a crushing silence. They are within twenty feet of the car and she has the remote raised, poised to unlock, when she finally collapses into his chest. Her head is ringing as though a bell has been struck inside her ear drum.

"Thank god, thank god."

He rubs her back and grins bashfully, like a man who has won something he didn't expect, which she supposes is the case in a way.

"Told you it was nothing."

She will allow this demonstration of bravado, which would normally have pricked at the always-eager-to-surface irritation. They already both feel a bit foolish about having spent the previous days worrying themselves sick, but even this feeling is a relief. They disengage from one another and she slaps his ass playfully as they perform their flanking maneuver on the car. Halfway to the vehicle he changes his mind.

"I'll drive."

She shrugs and tosses him the keys and they switch sides. As they pass the first sign listing their town she says, "Hey, maybe we should celebrate with dinner at the pizza place."

"The one Everett loves, with the crazy placemats?"

"Yeah."

"Sure. Be good to not have to cook."

She pulls out her phone and makes a call. "Hi, I'd like to make a reservation for three people. Around . . . " She glances at the illuminated time on the dashboard. "Eight?" She listens for a few seconds. "Oh? We didn't hear. OK, thanks for the tip. See you tonight."

She replaces the phone in her battered handbag. "They said there's a big thunderstorm heading our way. There's a surge warning for the whole coast."

He glances at her. "Should we call Ev?"

She nods and fishes the phone out again, presses the number and listens. "She's not answering."

"That's weird."

Astonishing how quickly the fear returns after being banished. The adrenaline floods back in like a king tide. Everett knows to always answer her phone. They haven't gone another two miles when the wind picks up so suddenly and violently. The car shudders and Paul has to make a hasty adjustment to keep driving in a straight line.

"Whoa."

On a normal day they might have already been aware of the climatic conditions. Of course, it hadn't been a normal day but still, this seems no longer like a valid excuse for leaving their young daughter alone. Yes, she's remarkably responsible for her age, and yes, they have vowed to be antihelicopter parents, and yes, their experimental rejection of the all-American diet of fear has, so far, exceeded their wildest dreams in terms of having raised a well-adjusted, open-minded child whose independence is a source of much pride and friend envy. But they both privately feel they would exchange all of that for the peace of mind that has now fled, leaving behind a howling paranoia. Paul presses his foot to the accelerator although they're already doing the speed limit, but she doesn't chastise him. It's not even five o'clock but the sky is already dark as a pit.

*   *   *

Everett doesn't hear about the storm coming but she feels it. After hours of roaming and beachcombing she's a long way from the boat when the wind starts howling. She squints at the sky. The scudding clouds are a color she's never seen before. For a moment her mind is a blank, then three white numbers appear: *000.* She tucks this knowledge away.

Within minutes a deluge has wiped out the world. She crouches in the scant shelter of a copse of ragged trees while she decides what to do. Soon she has it: she must try to rescue some of the eggs. She pulls her hood up, puts her head down, and runs back the way she came, toward the dunes. The sand is being lashed by the wind and rain: already the dunes have changed shape beneath the pummeling and the beach-grass is pressed completely flat. She raises a hand to protect her eyes while she rummages around in the sodden sand where she remembers seeing the nests. The rain is hard as pellets on the back of her neck. She finds only two eggs, and these she places carefully in each pocket of her sweatshirt, among the balled-up tissues and scraps of paper and hair ties furred with strands of her hair. She fancies she feels the warmth of the nesting eggs radiating through the fabric. It comes down in sheets like the rain in movies, and the solid state of it disorients her so that she can no longer be sure in which direction the marina lies. She isn't frightened exactly, but when she presses her thumb to her wrist she can feel her pulse galloping.

She pulls the hood closer around her face, and takes her phone from her back pocket and turns on the flashlight. It illuminates her hand and about three inches in front of her. She sees there are messages, probably from her parents, but that will have to wait until she's back on the boat. The thundering of the rain on the sand and the roar of the ocean just over the dunes doesn't just deafen her but bends every sense into disarray.

She takes a step to her right, sensing the marina that way, but she doesn't realize that the tiny rivulets of water where she some-times finds tadpoles have swelled into a churning stream in the downpour, and she loses her footing and goes down without a sound, all the air sucked out of her lungs. The water isn't deep but the current is strong and she struggles and splutters in the muddy water, trying to get a grip on the shifting banks, to lift herself up. When she finally staggers to her feet, mud sucking at her shoes, her hair all wild and sticking to her face, she realizes that she has lost the phone: it was ripped out of her hand when she fell, swept away toward the hungry ocean.

She waits for the jagged lightning to come. When it does, she yelps in distress at seeing she has veered far out of her way: instead of heading toward the marina she has come out on the other side of the peninsula, close to the wilder beach at which she's forbid-den to swim. There are no houses around here, yet she sees a light wavering through the rain. She perks up: it must be her parents out looking for her. But the light doesn't move, doesn't bob up and down like a flashlight, and as she moves closer she sees that it is fixed, and coming from a small dwelling on the sheltered side of a long low sand dune, half-obscured by panic grass.

As she approaches she hears a voice calling out and she begins to run, slipping with every few steps. Cal stands in the open doorway of the shack, waiting. She smells the rank, animal scent of his pipe, and sees the red glow of the embers like an evil winking eye as he sucks in. She raises a hand in greeting, so happy to see another living being, and slips past the door he is holding open for her.

*   *   *

Only after Caroline and Paul reach the boat and search its empty ringing spaces does the panic really take hold. They grab waterproof jackets and head back out into the storm, gripping each other as they run and search and call. They may as well be screaming underwater for all the sound carries. Everett isn't in any of the usual places, the places where there might be any kind of shelter from this wild weather. They knock on the doors of the nearest houses but all three are dark and no one comes. They look in the public-toilet block and the desolate bus station. They don't look in the water, though; not yet. Please god, not yet. Wind whips at their clothes. Their shoes are soaked through. Caroline is crying openly now, her mouth hanging open like cats when they're frightened.

"She's probably back at the boat by now!" he yells to her, although he doesn't believe this. "Let's go check."

Because he knows Caroline won't hear over the noise, he says the incantation out loud: "*Let her be there, let her be there.*" They stumble back along the pier and leap onboard, but apart from the sickening tilt of the deck beneath their feet nothing has changed, the vessel is still empty. They stand there for a moment in the downpour, unsure of what to do. It's already impossible to imagine ever being dry or warm or not terrified again. Caroline bows her head as if gathering strength.

"We should try that shack," she yells into his ear. "Cal's shack."

He nods with fevered intensity, relieved she hadn't suggested getting the police involved or summoning a search party. That would be acknowledging that she might really be lost, or worse. They want her to be at Cal's shack and dread it at the same time. They run all the way, splashing and cursing. Caroline goes down near the big sand dunes when her foot gets twisted in a root. One minute she's running beside him and the next she's sprawled facedown in the sand. Events seem to occur outside of ordinary physics.

"I'm alright, I'm alright," she pants as he pulls her up. She holds her hands in front of her like a penitent, and he sees her palms are grazed, pitted with tiny angry puncture marks. She holds onto him as they run, favoring her left leg a little, leaning into him. Finally they see it, a wavering light through the rain.

They hammer on his door while the rain in turn hammers down on the shack's tin roof like some unholy orchestra. We must look like sewer rats, Caroline thinks, capable even during crisis of experiencing anxiety at being unable to present their best selves. It feels like a long time before he opens the door, and she dreads what this could mean. Cal's body takes up the entire doorway. She hasn't ever noticed before how big he is, the muscular barrel of his chest and the angry flushed heft of his neck, where the edge of a blurry tattoo peeks coquettishly from his shirt collar. She marvels at the discrepancy between how fragilely he lives on the margins and how solidly he exists in the world. She in contrast feels hopelessly insubstantial, as if the molecules of her and her husband are in danger of simply being absorbed into the storm. Cal calmly contemplates their fevered faces, then steps aside so they can see into the cabin where their daughter sits wrapped in a grubby striped blanket in front of a radiator, reading *Little House on the Prairie*. She looks up and waves at them.

"Well, you may as well come in and have a drink. Look like you've seen a ghost."

It's just an expression, but they both feel an immense gratitude spread through them like warmth, not just that he has their daughter but that he really *sees* them, sees that they have seen the ghost of some terrible future and have been spared. Holding hands, they step inside the shack. The cacophony of the storm is instantly muffled, or perhaps it's just that the other sound makes the rain register as background. It's like nothing she's ever heard before, the song emitting from a pair of black beaten-up speakers. A bit like those Gregorian chants everyone was into for a while, but with something electronic and percussive behind it. Strange and haunting and beautiful in a way that makes tears prick in her eyes. They wrap themselves around their daughter, who squeals and wriggles away from their wetness, her little hands beating at their backs as she laughs. Paul laughs too, a little unhingedly. Then, in a kind of daze, they move away from her and sit down where Cal indicates—in maroon canvas folding chairs that sag like hammocks beneath them—and accept tumblers of vodka although neither of them drink spirits.

Caroline takes a sip of her drink and tries to be discreet as she looks around at Cal's home. He has divided the shack into three spaces using stretched cord and sheets of fabric. There's a tiny camp stove, a toaster oven and a kettle on packing crates in the kitchen; a futon-style mattress on a low wooden platform in the bedroom, with a stack of books next to it and a gooseneck lamp; and this room, with its folding chairs, card tables, and mismatched cushions. In one corner an open wooden tea crate is stacked neatly with fishing rods and nets. There are dozens of hooks on every wall, holding clothes, towels, hats, and black-and-white photographs of birds in roughhewn frames. There's something familiar and therefore comforting about the space, in its humble economy, perhaps because it reminds them both of living on a boat.

"Got you living over at the Smithside Marina, I heard?"

"Yep," says Paul, trying to sound jaunty and unashamed, although he wonders how Cal even knows where they live. "We stay there just over the summer. Then go back to our, ah, house for the rest of the year."

Cal laughs. "Didn't get invited to the party, huh?"

Paul smiles as if this doesn't sting. "Guess not."

"She doesn't look too seaworthy."

"I resent that," Caroline says, feeling lighthearted from the vodka and the heat and the nauseating relief. "I'm as seaworthy as the next woman. Oh, you mean the boat?"

The man stares at her for a long moment before a grin dawns and spreads across his face. "That's right. That's right. I knew you were good people."

She actually blushes at this. It is shameful how much she longs to be a good person. Each of them casts furtive glances at Everett, who is still engrossed in her book. Could he possibly have touched her, or even said anything inappropriate? What kind of middle-aged man keeps children's books around? The thought is like ice swallowed whole.

But Everett is happy as a clam, and they can both see there will be a minor meltdown when the time comes to leave. Sure enough, when the rain has stopped and they get up to leave, Everett juts her bottom lip out and begins whining. Caroline insists on collecting the glasses and taking them to the kitchen area. When she places them in the plastic bucket he uses as a sink, she sees on a low table a stack of ink drawings on paper. Glancing over quickly at the two men talking in the doorway, Paul reassuring Cal that the two of them will personally lobby against his eviction, she leans down to look closer: the top drawing is a sea of swirls and crosshatching, mostly abstract but for the occasional figurative form—what appears to be a tiger with horns, and a fish with a long, jagged bill. Like the music, they are beautiful and strange and a little discomfiting.

Cal's face turns stormy when they try to thank him, as if it's the one thing he can't abide.

"Don't carry on. You're welcome any time. And this one." He inclines his head toward Everett and she grins up at him like she would an old friend.

The entire world is dripping as they march in the sodden gloom back to the boardwalk. Everett bounces between them, each of them holding one of her hands.

"Can I visit Cal tomorrow?"

"We'll see," says Paul. "It was nice of him to look after you until we arrived, but we don't like you going there on your own."

"Why not?" A defiant quaver in the voice.

He sighs and Caroline can see he's too tired, wrung out and hollow after all the drama, to explain.

"Well honey," she says. "Because you know about stranger danger from school."

"He's not a stranger though. And he can see music."

What can this mean? She remembers the drawings in Cal's shack, and how their wild, slightly frightening vitality had reminded her of something. She sees now what it was: Everett's rare and odd gift for putting numbers to colors, like she has another eye inside her with which she sees the world. Instead of the worry she probably should feel at this insight, she is overcome with a surge of hope at the poignant thought that her daughter might someday find her people. That her daughter might have a people to find.

"Well, that's technically true. But we still have to be careful." She hesitates for a moment, wondering how much of the lecture to deliver. Sometimes it feels like they're just performing parenthood. "There are some men who can't be trusted around children."

"Because they're pervs?"

She stifles a smile: where had the child learned that word?

"Well yes, something like that. Because they're disturbed. They're sick."

She feels disloyal saying this after having spent time with Cal, who sees music and likes birds and seems to understand their daughter and her affinities on a level her parents have failed to.

"But Cal isn't sick. He's just sad."

"Well OK, that's as may be."

"But I want to give him this. I forgot." And the child stops, drops their hands, and rummages in her pocket, then opens her palm to reveal in the wavering flashlight glow a single tiny bird's egg, miraculously intact. "We talked about the sand nests and he visits them too."

Everett is tall for her age and too big to be carried, but on an impulse her mother sweeps her up anyway, gripping her around the thighs and grunting and staggering a little under the weight. She presses her head into the girl's damp belly and rubs her face from side to side, the wet cotton moving like a slug against her nose. Everett shrieks and squirms in her arms, and it takes a moment to understand what her loud protesting is about.

Caroline pulls her face away and looks up through the shadows at her daughter, whose right arm is thrust into the gaping sky, holding the egg far from her mother's body so it doesn't come to any harm.

EMMA SLOLEY is a journalist and fiction writer whose work has appeared in Catapult, Yemassee, *the* Tishman Review, Lunch Ticket, Structo, Travel + Leisure *and* New York *magazine, among many others. She is a MacDowell fellow and her debut novel,* Disaster's Children, *will be published by Little A books in Fall 2019. Born in Australia, Emma now divides her time between the US, Mexico, and various airport lounges. You can find her on Twitter @Emma_Sloley and www.emmasloley.com*

The Process

Rebekah Bergman

A *memory:* Here's Abe making Syl guess the next celebrity patient. "Who will it be?" he presses her. "Let's bet a dollar on it."

They are talking of Prosyntus, which has been available to the public since the first of the year. Wealthy actors are demanding it all in a rush. Not those who are freshly famous, but the ones whose names are already slipping to the tips of the tongue.

Here's Syl struggling to come up with a likely candidate. "Frederick Peters?" she guesses. As soon as she says it, she knows it is wrong. But why exactly?

"Who's Frederick Peters?" That's J.P., wanting to play the game with his parents.

"Frederick Peters?" Now Abe laughs gently. "But Frederick Peters is already dead."

*   *   *

Syl is eating breakfast at the kitchen counter. J.P. sits between her and Abe. The morning news is on their small TV above the fridge and an ad for Prosyntus plays during each commercial break. They eat without speaking.

Syl has hated the name Prosyntus since the beginning. It makes the procedure sound sterile and mythological while giving no clue as to what it really entails. Medical language is like that. It hides its meaning, withholds what it can do to your body. She and Abe have been calling it "The Process," but this is misleading as well. Prosyntus stops a process; it doesn't make one begin.

For a time, Prosyntus maintained its celebrity status. It was constant and yet removed from their normal existence. After the actors, the supermodels lined up to preserve their bodies at the peaks of their careers. Athletes came next, once the ethical questions about that had passed. But now, it is something anyone can have if they choose to. Syl tries to see why anyone chooses to. She pictures a future where she approaches death without aging, without changing. It is a hard image to hold onto. Her hair starts sprouting curly white wires, like springs loosened from a clock. Her spine bends into a question mark. This is how memory distorts imagination. It is impossible to empty the future of the past it is meant to contain.

J.P. reminds his parents that his class is taking a field trip later that week. The yearly trip to Marks Island. Syl will be chaperoning.

"I think you'll go into the Caves of Adina this time," Abe says.

J.P.'s eyes widen. "What are those?"

"I don't want to ruin the surprise," Abe says. "You'll see."

J.P. looks at Syl, anxious, and she pats his leg. "They aren't scary," she says. "You'll like them. You don't have to be scared."

J.P. is not his father. Syl would like to remind Abe of this for the hundredth time. He's not the way Abe was when Abe was a boy. Not that Syl knew Abe then, but she's heard his stories. Abe at ten, an intrepid explorer, hiking around Marks Island on his own. It was a new island then—newly old, that is, freshly discovered. Abe would climb into the Caves of Adina and through the passage that led to what had been a shore. He would stand out there and pretend he was one of the ancient people who'd made that place home. J.P. is sensitive and nervous by nature. Thoughtful and curious, like his father, but more of a worrier than his father ever has been.

A car beeps. It's Evangeline and her grandfather. J.P.'s carpool to school. He hops off the stool, kisses his parents, grabs his lunch from the counter, and leaves.

* * *

Syl is brushing her teeth when Abe tells her he will be having The Process. It isn't the first time he's said it. The first time he said it she was stunned into silence. And the second time she decided Abe was kidding. He had to be. She jutted her chin out like a small child and teased him.

"Okay," she said then, "Maybe there's a two-for-one discount. We can both have it. Maybe J.P. should have it done too."

"You're joking," Abe replied. "But I'm not."

This time, he has made his appointment. He speaks of logistics. When it's over, will Syl be able to meet him at the Facility? The appointment is scheduled for Friday. Someone will need to sign for him, to drive him home. Can she do that?

Syl wants to protest. To scream. To throw a tantrum. To make it stop. But it is too late. Abe has made up his mind, like crossing a threshold. Their reflections catch eyes in the mirror. Yes, she tells Abe, she can.

* * *

It is Syl's turn to make dinner. J.P. is helping roll out the pizza dough. He dips his hands into a bag of flour. When he pulls them out, they are the hands of a ghost. Syl needs to tell him about his father. She doesn't want to, really, but she should. Their son, in any case, deserves to know.

She could start with, "It is a choice your father has made for his body." Or, "It has nothing to do with you or with me." Neutral, journalistic language. The only problem is that it should. It should have everything to do with them. Shouldn't it? And then again, maybe it does.

She chops vegetables and J.P. arranges them on the pizza, making a face with mushroom eyes. He is so young, their son. His family must still seem like an extension of his body, his self. He hasn't yet realized that this life was in no way inevitable. Parents, for instance. Most parents do not have a wide gap of time between them.

Abe is older than Syl is. Nineteen years older. It is longer than the lifespan of a family pet. J.P. must not yet see this gap or how it forms a fault line between his mother and father. Syl expects J.P. to ask over his cornflakes any morning now why Evangeline's grandfather is the age of his dad.

"Mom," J.P. says. He is setting the table. "Wednesday's the field trip. Please don't forget."

Has she ever forgotten?

Yes. Once. Twice. She makes a note and tapes it to the cabinet. Just two words: *Don't forget.*

*   *   *

"It does not postpone death or prevent sickness. Remember that," a famous artist is saying. She's being interviewed on the news station where Syl works.

The artist, Monique Gray, has been a strong voice against The Process. Syl can see several images of Gray at the same time. One is real—she is small and faces forward—the others are projected and enlarged from so many angles on so many screens. Two of Gray's ex-husbands have had The Process. Her current boyfriend is about to have it done too. Gray is adamant that it is a setback for civilization. She speaks of life cycles and mythology and how humans are born to die and will always die and it's unnatural and immoral to pretend it can be some other way.

"We are fooling ourselves," she says. "We are fools."

The host asks about the billboards by the highway.

"Those?" she says. "Yes, I've seen them. They fill the air like locusts."

On each billboard, there is a portrait of a gorgeous celebrity who's had The Process. Their features, so symmetrical they look alien.

"We need to remember," Gray says, "Prosyntus has not made them this beautiful. Fame and money have done that. We forget this. Although yes, it's true, Prosyntus will keep them there. They won't age."

On the billboards, the year is written in the corner in large, bold script.

"So I get it," she says, "no matter when you see these ads, you know as you speed past, that the people in the ads will still look the same. It's powerful," she says. "It's persuasive."

The host nods. He's been very quiet in this interview.

"But we've got to remember: it's not time travel. It's not magic. It just numbs a body from pain, blocks any changes, up to the point when it reaches its end. It stops symptoms so you can forget about death, but death will still happen. One day, you—like everyone else—will be dead."

She stops there, lets that sink in.

"I see," the host says. He turns to the camera, smiles. "Stay with us. We'll be right back."

Syl leaves the set and heads to her office. It will be difficult to fact-check Gray's interview. The Process is still largely a secret. Still, Gray's basic sentiment about it is true. It prevents aging and change but it does not stop death. After The Process, a body will die without suffering, without pain—but it will still die.

For a second, Syl envisions a world where death is nothing more than that. Nobody can tell when a person is dying, not even that person himself. So a woman is buying orange juice in the grocery store. A man is getting a haircut. A wife is kissing a husband, a son. And then, in an instant, all those people are gone.

*   *   *

A memory: Here's Abe and here's Syl two years into their marriage, just after J.P. is born. Here's Syl thinking that they've managed to bridge the distance between them, cross over it, that those nineteen years are behind them and they are free to march forward together onto new ground.

And here's Abe feeling a sickness inside his body. Here's Syl driving Abe to a doctor who confirms what they both know. Here's a full year of his body and its unchanging illness. He is sick in the autumn, sick in the winter, sick in the spring. When summer comes back around, Abe is still sick.

Here's Syl caring for Abe and caring for J.P. who is just a baby and may never remember his father at all, let alone as a healthy man. And here's the feeling underneath all the other feelings that this is the end of their story. Whether it ends now or later, this is the way it will end. There is no acceptance or denial about that. It is merely an awareness of something just uncovered, a buried truth that was there all along.

And then, another autumn, and here's Abe getting well. Here's the color coming back to his face, the strength to his limbs, the blue to his pale eyes. Here's Syl believing that the ending is not happening now but knowing, still, that someday that ending will come. Here's Abe racing J.P. around the backyard. Here's J.P. poking his head up from a pile of leaves and Abe jumping into it. And here's Syl clinging to one small hope from this moment forward: that when it does happen, they will know it is happening. It won't make it better and it won't make her less scared, but they will be able to help each other because they will know.

*   *   *

Syl spends the day coordinating a special broadcast for the fiftieth anniversary of Marks Island. Not the land itself, but the discovery of it.

Everyone is fascinated by Marks Island. Though no one alive knew this land when it was an island at all. That was close to ten thousand years ago. As time passed, the sea level fell, and a narrow strip connected the island to the motherland like an umbilical. For generations, the past was erased by an isthmus. The city grew with all its people, and none of them thought twice about the bit of land that jutted out into the ocean. Nobody asked why the city was shaped like a lowercase *i* with the dot never fully separated from the line but coming close at high tide.

Abe was J.P.'s age when Francis Marks found a cave with human remains in it, and then the truth of their geography washed over them. Abe said it was a phenomenon. News crews came to the beach to report on the finding. Syl loved this, the past being reported as news, everybody learning about where they came from, what their land had once contained. Abe loved it, too. He said it was the main reason that he had become a historian.

This special broadcast will include an interview with Francis Marks's oldest grandson. He owns the museum on Marks Island, heads a preservation committee and does a lot of work with youth. Syl has been reading the interview over and over. She has completely lost track of time.

"Who would you recommend visit the museum?" the reporter asks.

"Everyone," he says. "Everyone should visit it. We get caught up in the future. We end up not noticing what's slipping behind. It's nice to look at artifacts every now and then, isn't it? To spend a few moments inhabiting a place that is filled with the past."

*   *   *

Every year, the same field trip. The same sticky bus seats with rips in the backs and duct tape crossed over them. The same windows that open like jawbones and hurt the pads of fingers to unlock.

Syl sits beside J.P. who is not too old yet to sit with his mother instead of his friends.

"What do birds do when it rains?" he asks. Syl has no idea why he is asking. There are no birds in the parking lot. There are no signs of rain. She often thinks that J.P. hoards his questions until they have enough time together to air them out.

It is thirty-five minutes to Marks Island. They play bus games. The children sing call-and-response songs, filling the bus with a synchronized shouting. The rituals of fourth graders. They clap hands on laps to keep the rhythm. One song is about Marks Island. A memory: Syl singing this same song in grade school.

"Have you been to Marks?" ("Yes, ma'am.")

"How did you get to Marks?" ("I swam.")

"When was your journey?" ("Back twelve years.")

"What was it like there?" ("Not like here.")

"That's how you get to Marks."

In each verse, the same questions are met with new responses. The journey becomes more and more recent. They get there by boat, by bridge, by road, and, finally, they just walk right over. The island becomes increasingly familiar with each repetition. It is a strange land, an odd place, a quaint spot until, in the last verse, what was it like there? Just like here.

If Abe were a chaperone on this field trip, he would not remember this song from his own childhood. This is how their gap of time becomes a distance. Years between are years apart, years that separate. She feels it in the bits of history she studied in school that Abe lived through. In the words of slang she peppers into conversation that he needs her to translate. In his own idioms, too, with their archaic violence: skinning cats, stoning birds. Where did he come from with such phrases? They clash so harshly with his kind, pale eyes.

When Marks Island was really an island, people lived there. All alone, they may have evolved independently.

"No, it was certainly *not* divergent evolution." Here's a tour guide at the museum correcting Syl an hour later. He speaks in a monotone that still manages to sound condescending. "Not at all," he explains. "Divergent evolution would take a much, much longer time."

Okay, so not diverging from other humans. Just living alone then.

This year, just like Abe thought, the Caves of Adina are open. The caves have been damaged by flooding, so they must divide into groups of five and take turns going in. Syl stays above ground. She does not need to see the caves. She's seen them before.

"You're not coming?" J.P. asks.

"No," she says. "But you'll like it down there. It's neat."

These are the caves that Francis Marks discovered and named for his wife. They were either ancient tunnels that partially filled in or else burial grounds for the people of Marks Island. There are several theories. The remains of an ancient old man with a chronic ailment were found there though. That was one big discovery. This man suffered a degenerative joint condition. It was one of the most important findings of the whole excavation. "Like an ancient arthritis," Abe had told Syl once.

*   *   *

A memory: Here are Abe and Syl visiting the caves as a young couple. Here's Abe acting as if the remains of that man were dug up yesterday, or even still being dug up today. History is that alive to him.

"To survive at all, he needed the help of his tribe, Syl. He was in his mid-forties when he died." This is the fact Abe finds most exciting. "Forty-four, maybe forty-five." It's a remarkable age for such an early human. Did she understand that? "Like being over one hundred today."

So a sick man lived for a long time a long time ago. Why was that so groundbreaking?

"Further evidence of altruism among early man." Abe says, sounding like a research paper. "Do you see? For years, his tribe helped him survive. They had to lift him to help him down there. They say it supports the theory that altruism is inherently human."

"I don't think it was altruistic." Syl responds. She is thinking aloud. "Not necessarily. I don't think we can say that for sure."

"We can say that," Abe again. "Trust me. We can."

He has this frustrated tone that irks her, as if she is not under-standing instead of just disagreeing with him. And who is this "we" he is suddenly speaking for?

Syl doesn't think she should have to explain but she tries anyway. "Abe," she says, "think about us. If you were in pain and I helped you, it wouldn't be for you and you only, would it? If I'm helping you to not suffer, isn't that also for me?"

This resonates, she can tell. But he doesn't want to concede on his version of humanity. It is a beautiful, compelling version. But that doesn't make it true.

"I don't think so," he says. "I don't think it would still be for you."

A new feeling then, being at odds with each other. They do not speak for a time and when they do speak, the fight flares back up. It is an exhausting cycle.

"All I'm saying," she tries later, "is that people have all sorts of reasons for doing anything."

"So?" Abe almost laughs, not seeing what this has to do with the subject.

"So I don't think altruism is something a stranger can recognize in you. And especially not one from so long ago. I think it's one of those things, Abe," she says, "like memory. A thing you cannot really share with anyone else."

He smiles a real smile. "That's a very Syl point to make."

Abe is always noting this aspect of Syl. What he calls her belief in a "true human loneliness." It's a large reason why he loves her the way that he does. He wants to inhabit that emptiness at the core of her. But if he could, then it would be lost.

And that's it. Their first fight. They are both so relieved when it is over that they don't notice that it hasn't been resolved. There is no answer to the question of altruism. They can drop it, but it will not go away.

*   *   *

The bus back to school is quiet. They drive toward the sun and the kids close their eyes. Some fall asleep. J.P. had not been afraid of the Caves of Adina for long. He'd resurfaced from the depths with a group of three friends who he stayed with for the rest of the day.

Now, J.P. rests his head on her shoulder. They pass the billboards for The Process but it is too bright to see them. She feels the spiral of J.P.'s ear by her collarbone. He is so young. Here are his little legs on the bus seat. His feet. She pictures Abe's feet then as if she is holding them. Their incredible flatness. If Abe were a caveman, he would have died young. He could not have outrun anything. Poor man. It is not just the shape of the bones, but the level plane of skin that wraps around them. They are always cold like slabs of marble. She loves Abe's feet, loves touching them, though she knows that their flatness causes him great pain.

J.P. will turn eleven soon. One day his age will match the gap between Abe and Syl. A strange image of J.P. as the bridge that connects them. Stranger to think J.P. hasn't always been there. Since even before there was J.P., there was the idea of him.

A memory: Their first apartment, hers and Abe's. It is a dim basement with cardboard boxes stacked in small towers for lack of floor. Here's the damp smell of it, masked by candles. Here are Syl's hands on Abe's feet, rubbing in slow circles. It might be daybreak or midafternoon. There are no windows. Here are Syl's wrinkled palms against Abe's smooth, smooth soles. She is savoring that creamy softness. It reminds her of a baby they haven't yet had. Imagination is so close to memory. When you picture the future hard enough, it can feel like the past.

* * *

Syl is in her office, reading the introduction to a news segment.

"What happens when time is blocked off? When everything is preserved as it is?" the host asks. For a moment, Syl confuses this with the special broadcast on Marks Island. She skims the page. No, this is about The Process. She starts over and reads from the top.

The subject is a young man, young to have had Prosyntus, just thirty-two. He says he has lost the ability to remember since the procedure.

"I gave up my past," this man tells the reporter.

The reporter asks, "But you had Prosyntus. Wasn't that what you were trying to do?"

The poor man, Syl thinks. No, it was not.

At first, spokespeople for Prosyntus issued a statement about this man. Their procedure couldn't have any effect on long-term memory whatsoever. They went so far as to imply that the young man was delusional or else out for money and making it up. But other patients started coming forward with the same claim, and Prosyntus issued a new statement: forgetfulness was a sign of a serious but extremely rare side effect. The young man won a hefty lawsuit.

"The money doesn't matter," he explains. "I just want my life back."

Syl imagines the pain of this man's confusion. She knows it well. Her own mother began the process of dying by losing her memory, losing her connection to time altogether. Once, her mother had asked the doctor, "Who is the president of the country today?" and they all had a good, sad laugh about that. Sometimes, she did not know which language to speak. She kept forgetting that her husband was dead and this fact was newly devastating for her to learn.

Her mother's body was still healthy, still strong. But eventually, forgetting became a kind of cave that she lived inside. It kept her out of the blinding brightness of today. Why did she have to know for certain how the world had changed since she was a child? She knew, with certainty, that she once was a child who lived in the world. Wasn't that enough?

A memory: Here's her mother, looking the way she always looked. That is, warm, large, physically healthy—and yet, dying. Here's Syl pretending to be her mother's mother because that's what her mother believes.

"Mom," her mother says, holding onto Syl's hand.

"Mom," Syl repeats inside her head, holding on until her mother lets go.

*   *   *

At her desk, Syl quizzes herself for a few minutes. She imagines Abe without looking at his photograph. Discrete pieces. The square shape of his thumbnails, the smooth border of his hairline, the thin fold that wraps around the skin of his neck. She can build him from memory this way if she wants to. Bit by bit. But why would she want to? There will be no need to. Not anymore. Not even if, like her mother, she starts forgetting. Abe will always look the same after The Process. So there will be nothing for her to long for or miss. Only all of him, later.

Did Abe look younger when she'd first met him? She doesn't think so. When they had sex for the first time, something was wrong with Abe's left knee. She remembers his joint creaking more than the bedsprings. Hearing it, they couldn't help but laugh. And then the third time or the fourth when she had naively assumed that the awkward part was behind them, that they'd managed to place their bodies together and even laughed while doing it. When she rolled onto his left leg, just slightly, and his pale blue eyes filled up with pain. There it was: that distance. Here's Syl saying sorry, pulling away from him. Abe swallowing, breathing hard, swallowing again. Their bodies lying parallel, not touching for a long moment. The feeling of vertigo looking down from the bed. These fragments that blend to become our memory.

"Abe," she had said last night before falling asleep. "How will we know how much time we have together?"

"We won't," he told her. His voice was like water. "But Syl," he said, "we never could."

After Abe's illness and Syl's mother's death, she'd begun collecting mementos of their life together. The plastic souvenirs from their honeymoon, for instance, she dug them up and put them on a shelf and reminded Abe how they came to possess them, those three neon hula-dancer figurines. She could still remember. For some reason, Syl thinks of this now. How she took the photo album from their wedding—a book of frozen smiles and blurs of movements—and wrote down every guest's name. How she'd made a dozen home movies documenting J.P. as a baby: J.P. saying nonsense; J.P. eating mushed fruit; J.P. doing nothing remarkable, just lying on his back in his crib blowing bubbles of spit. They never watch these home movies now. But the point was never to watch them. The point had been to make them exist.

*   *   *

Back home, it is Abe's turn to make dinner and Syl sits, just watching him.

"What's going on?" J.P. asks as he enters the kitchen. It is too quiet.

"Nothing," Syl says. Though clearly, there is something. Abe drops a knife and it clangs against the floor.

"J.P.," Abe says, serving each of them salad from a large bowl, "tell me about the field trip."

J.P. lights up and starts talking. He is caught on one small detail—a geologic timeline at the museum. Abe eats, grabbing a dinner roll in each bear-like paw, and the meal becomes a typical family dinner, like thousands of others. Syl thinks they will confuse and forget the details of this one particular night.

She hadn't even noticed the geologic timeline that J.P.'s describing. She'd been too busy learning the mechanism of human evolution. Relearning it since, surely, she had known it all once. And what is the evolutionary advantage of forgetting? There must be one, but she cannot imagine what it could be.

The geologic timeline measures the history of the planet by the layers of fossils found in the rock. These, J.P. says, can be read like tree rings. Abe finds a pen from a junk drawer and gives J.P. a fresh napkin.

"Draw it for us," he says.

J.P. draws a circle, which is surprising. Syl had been expecting a line. He divides the perimeter of the circle in two.

"These are eons," J.P. tells them, "the largest units of time."

He draws arcs that go around the circle on the outside, concentric. Shorter than the hemispheres below. "Next are the eras."

Another series of arcs, above the last, shorter still, with almost no curve. "Then periods." Another, still shorter. "Epochs."

And finally, no more arcs, just one vertical line. It touches the surface of the original circle at a single point, "And this is an age, the smallest unit of time."

Typical Abe. He knows all this and is eager only to capture his son's interest and open it wide. He takes the napkin and places it next to the salad bowl, a centerpiece. "Look," he says and starts to lecture.

He speaks of Marks Island. Of the span of time when it existed as an island. It is immeasurably small. How, if the distance from his nose to the tip of his hand were the life of this planet, then a stroke on a nail file would erase human history entirely. And isn't that something?

Abe doesn't notice J.P. hunching over his plate. He doesn't stop to ask if J.P. is okay. J.P. is not okay. He hates when his father does this. Syl waits for J.P. to yell out or cry. But he doesn't. He clenches his jaw and stares at his lap. His feet rest on the floor, flat.

"The thing about this timeline," Abe concludes at long last, "is that it's relative. Every span of time is bound by a major event—a mass extinction, for instance, the age of the dinosaur. It is not absolute. They call it *deep time*," he says. "Did you know that, J.?"

"Mmm," J.P. says. Then he gets up to clear the table.

"Thanks," Abe calls, catching Syl's eye.

"You can leave it in the sink," Syl tells him. "Finish your homework, please."

Only the two of them in the kitchen. Abe's hair almost glows it is so white. Syl doesn't know when exactly it became that color, but it happened. It was always happening.

She is angry with Abe for making J.P. feel so little so quick, but Abe preempts her. "I know," he says. He looks bewildered. "I'm sorry. I got carried away."

They've never built a good method for fighting. There'd been that one lasting argument about the ancient old man. Before that, eons ago, there was mild bickering over the boundaries of their shared existence. Someone's dirty socks falling short of the hamper, the crescents of clipped toenails littering the bathroom floor. It was almost nice, those bodily signs of their life together.

So Abe is sorry. Good, but why is he telling her? He should tell J.P.

"I know," Abe says again. "I need to tell him."

Only after he is gone does Syl wonder what Abe is telling J.P. That he is sorry for the lecture or that he is having The Process, or both? That the appointment is just hours away now?

J.P.'s drawing is still on the table. There's the wobbly nature of J.P.'s writing. The arcs around the circle look like a pulse. Like a beating heart at the core of the Earth. A shred of lettuce has fallen onto it. Syl peels it off.

An age. It is the only time they are going to have, she and Abe. Just a slice of one. And this is it, right now. They are living in it. The Age of Sylvia and Abraham. What major event would mark their ending? There will be no way now to predict.

* * *

Here it is: The day of Abe's Process. On the cabinet, a sticky note with two words, "Don't forget." And she won't. She hunts for details to remember so she can trace it all back later to now.

"Wake up, Syl." That's Abe's voice. "Wake up," he says. "It's a beautiful day." He has been saying this forever, since they lived in the basement with no view of the sky. He'd say it, facing their square of white ceiling and Syl would laugh and ask, "How can you tell?"

Here's one of Abe's feet grazing her bare legs below the covers. Flat, smooth. Here's a flash of nightmare—touched by something she does not recognize, something lifeless, and yet, not dead.

What else? The tie he is wearing at breakfast. The swirling pattern on it. The gallon of milk on the counter. It has passed its expiration but it smells like nothing at all.

"Abe," Syl says to his back as he rinses the dishes. He does not hear her but she is asking if he is scared.

And in the future, what will she remember? After that gallon of milk is depleted, another one filling its place on the door of the fridge? Later still, after that tie begins to fray at the edges, the result of a single loose thread? How will imagination distort this memory?

This evening she will meet J.P. at practice. She will stand outside the gymnasium waiting for him. The dribbles will echo like a hundred heartbeats inside her chest. And she will remember that.

* * *

There is the drive to work. The view from the office. The ache in her wrists while she is typing. The mundaneness of her job, which could be any job, on this day, which could be any day. But it is not any day. Because she is here while Abe is at the Facility and this is the moment when things begin changing. The moment when things stop changing at all.

There is still work that needs to be done and she is still doing it. Tonight is the anniversary broadcast. Fifty years of Marks Island. Updated copies fly to her desk.

There is a segment on the tribe that lived on the island. Syl has questions that the piece does not answer. How did it feel to live with that old man among them? To help him for so many years. Was it a burden? Probably. But not enough of a burden to stop helping him, certainly not. And if they could change it, would they choose to? Or did they accept it without thinking that their lives could be any way else? Suddenly, it is dark and Syl needs to pick up J.P.

The drive is a blurred strip of asphalt that Syl does not remember because here she is already at school. The gym door swings shut heavily.

"Hi, Mom."

J.P. is wearing a knee brace.

"What happened?" Syl asks.

"Nothing happened," he tells her. "It just hurts."

As they near home, things slow down. There are J.P.'s eyes in the rearview. Pale blue, just like Abe's. She wishes that they looked more like her own—deep, dark pits in shades of brown soil. She sighs and begins telling him what his father has done, is doing. Healthy preteen sweat fills the car. That smell, she thinks, will coat this moment for both of them in retrospect.

J.P. interrupts her. "He told me, Mom. Dad told me. I already know. It's okay." The scene she imagined has become inverted: J.P. is the one comforting her.

"But, Mom," J.P. says. "I want to come with you."

The drive to the Facility will be the end of a chapter. Syl imagined she'd be alone first, then with Abe, then the three of them all together again. It is the right order for the next chapter to start.

J.P. sits on his fingertips, seatbelt still on. His voice cracks when he says, "Please."

"No, J.," Syl says. She knows this is selfish. "Trust me. You should wait at home. We'll be back in an hour. Okay?"

J.P. unbuckles and walks to the front door. He turns back, looks at Syl, and waves.

* * *

The Facility is a monolith with very few windows. The waiting room is uncomfortably bright. On TV, a teaser for the anniversary broadcast. There are the bones of the ancient, sick man. Syl thinks of his tribe, how they carried him into the safety of the cave like it was a womb. Did he feel helpless? Syl wonders.

Forty-four, it was a remarkable age for an early human, the host is saying.

Yes, Syl knows, like one hundred today. But did he have a wife? Was she younger than he was? Children? Maybe one child they had not been expecting but who had nonetheless come? Had she pictured the future of her husband's ailment? Was it a fundamental piece of the person she was? Even so, picturing it couldn't have shaped how it happened. She must have discovered that.

Abe appears from nowhere and stands beside her. She gets up and they kiss.

"That was the first kiss of the rest of our lives," Syl says. She means this to be funny, but it comes out flat.

"How do you feel?" She clears her throat.

"Great," he says.

Syl says, "Good." She kisses him to replace the first one that has turned stale already. He takes his bag, she signs the form, and then they leave. On their way home, the highway is wide and empty, stretching on and on and on.

* * *

J.P. does not come running to the door when he hears the car park. They find him sitting in the living room with the TV turned down.

"J.," Abe says.

J.P.'s eyebrows lift. "Dad," he says. "You're okay?"

Abe sits down beside his son. "I'm okay."

J.P. stares at Abe and Abe stares at J.P. and they hug. Syl finds the remote and turns the volume up. It is the ending of a movie they've all seen before. J.P. and Abe are talking, low and fast, laughing together, relieved. But Syl doesn't listen. She's forgotten the premise of the film. Who are these characters? How are they related? Why are they doing the things that they do?

The three of them stay up late. J.P. eats leftover fries from a Styrofoam container. He sits on the floor with his back against the couch. Abe reaches over to grab a handful, but drops them because they're cold.

"Ew," Abe complains. "How can you eat them like that?"

J.P. faces forward. "Like what?" he eats two at once. "They taste good." There is ketchup globbed on J.P.'s chin like too-bright blood.

"J.P.," Abe says, "wipe your face."

J.P. sticks his tongue out and licks it off.

"J.P., please," Syl says. It may be the first thing she's said since they came home.

The late-night news is on and she and Abe watch it after J.P. goes to bed. Monique Gray has just had The Process. The news anchors do not know what to make of this development.

A commercial break. A supermodel speaks of her life since The Process. What her skin-care regime looks like now.

"So," Syl says, searching for something else they can talk about. Anything else. The supermodel's teeth are blank slates when she smiles.

"So," Abe says. "So it's not that different, right? So maybe it'll never be different again."

*   *   *

Some memories: Nineteen years. It was always there. And yet. The day Abe had The Process. All the details she forgot and then wrote over. The palimpsest of memory. How they returned to the Caves of Adina. How they fought without fighting, without even approaching their situation, their selves.

"That ancient man," Syl saying, "his suffering is what kept him alive. Because his tribe knew about it. So they helped him. And so he lived."

"And his tribe?" Abe asking. "What good did his suffering do for his tribe?"

The pattern on his tie. How it made her dizzy. The vertigo of looking down from the bed when she'd caused him pain. How his body would no longer anchor her to any one clear time at all. And what would happen when she began to forget him?

"Death," Abe saying, "It's one of those things, Syl. Pain too. Things that cannot be shared." How he sounded almost happy, like he finally understood something.

How this conversation brought Syl back to their baby. To J.P. when he was brand-new, a minute old, when he did not yet have a name. And backward from that point, to being in labor, to the pain like a solid wall that, without warning, would crumble around her and be forgotten as soon as it was gone. While for J.P., it had all been so simple. Like crossing a threshold.

"Why not make it easier?" Abe saying.

Easier for whom? That should have been her next question. But she thought she knew and did not have to ask.

*　　*　　*

Here's Syl, her hair has lost its pigment and her brown eyes have fogged so they look more like dust than soil. Life has continued and nothing has changed except for once, when there was a choice before her. When that gap was closed and it was time for her to make up her mind. She could seal the nineteen years forever. Fall asleep in a sterile room and wake up with no space between them at all. She did not do it. She wanted her body to help her remember as her mind continued to forget and forget.

She is older than Abe is now. That is, her body has grown older than his ever will. Does she regret this? Sometimes she does. Sometimes she does not. Mostly, she is lost in a deep time where there is no Process. She is in their first apartment. She is holding their baby. She is rubbing her wrinkled hands on someone else's skin—whose skin is that? It is so smooth. How did it get so smooth?

J.P. is a man and not even a young one. He's tall and thin like his father, the same bad knees, the same flat feet. When Syl looks at her son, she can see the man she fell in love with. When she looks for the man she fell in love with, she cannot find him. Where is the man she was supposed to grow old with?

Here's Syl holding a very small child. "It's going to be a beautiful day," someone is saying. Who is saying that? "Wake up," he says. And she should, she knows. She should wake up. She is trying to.

Here's that strange, sudden earthquake that hit their town some years back. All the felled trees, the rings of the trunks sliced open, exposed. The real damage was on Marks Island. The isthmus was severed in a rare event, the tide rising so fast and hard it cut through the land. So Marks Island is an island again.

Syl imagined the ancient man when it happened. It was him, she thought, digging through the land-bridge. Why would he do that? She could not say. There were so many reasons people did anything. Weren't there? Anyway, she could see him, that old man. She can see him still.

Here he is, bending low with a shovel. His pale eyes sparkling. Here are his feet, two stones of marble. And the creak of his bad knee rolls over to her, echoing, from across a new sea.

REBEKAH BERGMAN's *stories have been published in* Hobart, Joyland, Nashville Review, Conium Review, Cosmonauts Avenue, Necessary Fiction, *and* Passages North, *among other journals. She studied writing at Brown University and earned an MFA in fiction from The New School. Rebekah has received residencies and fellowships from Art Farm and Tent Creative Writing. She was a 2018 Tennessee Williams Scholar at the Sewanee Writers' Conference. She lives in Brooklyn and is at work on a novel. For more, visit rebekahbergman.com.*

The Collectors of Anguish

Andrea Uptmor

Marcy was a fat twelve-year-old. Many people told her this: her twin brother Robert, who, though stout himself, had established enough popularity at school via basketball skills and dirty jokes to counteract any shame that came with being overweight; her classmates, who drew bulbous piglets on her paper lunch bag with sharpies; and most of all, her mother Ruth, who sliced Marcy's hamburgers in half with a butter knife and followed her into the dressing room at Penney's, where she frowned and pinched the bubble of tummy that emerged over crisp new blue jeans.

Marcy had a theory for a while that this was the reason her mother disappeared to New York. To get away from her, from the fat.

But when she got up the nerve to finally ask, her father said: no, of course not, it was for other reasons. He popped the bubbles that appeared in the pancake batter as it cooked. Then he set the spatula down and pressed his thumbs into his eyelids. He said: "How could you even think that, honey?"

* * *

Ruth had grown up in New York City, a place Marcy imagined as a huge gymnasium full of silver buildings and cars that honked in a loud, painful chorus. Ruth had come to college in the Midwest on a dance scholarship, and that's where she met Marcy's father, Bruce, who in those days had a long beard and wrote sonnets about the way the moonlight cast shapes like rivers on her belly as she danced. They got married, and when she got pregnant, they gave up their artistic pursuits together: her father went to the police academy, and her mother took a job at the bank. And that's how they came to spend their middle age in Lovington, where Marcy and Robert could walk down the middle of the road on the way to school, kicking their backpacks ahead of them like soccer balls.

Sometimes when Ruth told this story it sounded romantic, and she grew misty-eyed when she talked about the hands of fate pulling her toward the man of her dreams. Other times she spoke of it as if she had been held hostage, and when she was in that sort of mood, nothing tasted good, and sometimes she disappeared to her room right in the middle of dinner.

"What did I do wrong?" Marcy would ask.

"Nothing," her father would say and pat her hand. "Nobody did."

*   *   *

That spring, Marcy was listening to music and braiding the loose fringe on the edge of her blanket when Ruth burst in, plucked the headphones from Marcy's ears, and dropped a plastic bag on the bed. "Guess who signed up for a year of ballet lessons?" She spun around twice, her long braid whipping around her head.

"You?"

Ruth stopped spinning. She put her hands on her hips. "No, goofus. *You.*"

"But I don't want to do ballet lessons."

"Of course you do."

Marcy pictured herself squeezed into a leotard, galloping across a stage like a horse. "Please don't make me."

"You start on Thursday. If you don't make a fuss, we'll go to dinner afterward."

"Everyone?"

"Just me and you," her mother said over her shoulder as she went downstairs. From the window Marcy watched her mother stride across the freshly cut lawn, pause at the street to bend down and touch her toes, and then turn down Pine Street toward the park. It was her nightly tradition, this walk, and she did it even in the cold of winter. She called it her head-clearing time.

Marcy opened the bag. Inside were three pairs of pink tights, a pink leotard, and a crisp pink pair of ballet shoes. She shut her door and tried them on. In the mirror she looked like a swollen mosquito bite.

Robert entered, flushed and sweaty from playing soccer with the neighbors, and confirmed this fact.

*   *   *

Later: "Whoo-hoo," her father said. He was balancing the checkbook, writing their expenses in neat blue letters and folding over each page. He peered at her over the rim of his glasses. "A ballerina just like her mom."

"Not quite," Ruth said. She pinched the lip of fat beneath Marcy's butt to make her point.

*   *   *

The ballet classes were held in a blue metal building at the edge of the city. "The girls will be younger than you," her mother said as they arrived. "That's because you're a late bloomer. Most girls start dancing when they're six or seven."

"Is that how old you were?" Marcy asked, hoping to delay getting out of the car. She watched a woman hold the door open for her daughter, whose hair was pulled back in a neat bun with ribbons.

"I was five. My mother was very resourceful. We didn't have a lot of money, but she had a whole tailoring business just to pay for the lessons." She tapped her fingers on the wheel. "You're such a lucky girl."

"I know."

"Do you?" Her mother squinted at her, pursed her lips. The sun glinted in the window, casting a yellow line across her face.

Marcy squinted and pushed thoughts of gratitude into her head: her pink bicycle with the basket on the handlebars, *Alf*, French fries, days that went by without a single stomachache. "Yes," she said.

"Well, go on inside, then, while I park."

*   *   *

Her mother was right—the other girls in the class were younger. Marcy towered over them, yet she couldn't quite keep up with the moves. The teacher was a frowning woman with swinging earrings and short hair who kept putting her hands on Marcy's stomach.

"Tummy in," she said.

She put her hands on Marcy's rear end, too.

"Derriere in," she said.

The worst part was the mirror—it covered an entire wall, so it became impossible for Marcy to avoid seeing the desperate buckling of her body as it tried to mimic the other girls. Her mother watched through a window that joined the studio to the lobby. Whenever Marcy took her eyes off the mirror, they would fall upon her mother's face, framed in the window, as she tapped out the rhythm of the music on the sill.

Stand up straight, she would mouth, elongating her own posture. Suck your tummy in.

*   *   *

Later, while Ruth was gone, Marcy asked her father why her mother didn't dance anymore.

He turned off the faucet and put the last of the bowls in the dish drainer. "She wasn't good enough," he said, wiping his hands on a towel. "But don't you ever repeat that."

*   *   *

As promised, every Thursday her mother took her to a diner on the edge of town after lessons. They ate salads, Ruth's choice, and Marcy picked out the croutons and ate them first. She wished she could savor things like her mother, who pushed them off to the side and ate them last, when Marcy's plate was already clean and she could only watch with longing.

"You have a clean arabesque," Ruth said one night. She had a dab of dressing on the corner of her mouth, and instinctively her tongue flicked out and removed it. "But your grand plié tends to buckle as it deepens. You have to keep your back straight."

"But it hurts."

"Ballet hurts. That's part of the deal."

"What deal?"

"The deal of becoming graceful. Beautiful." Ruth waved her hand to the waiter for the check, her bracelets clattering together, and cocked her head at her daughter. "Dear, you're going to need a bra soon."

*   *   *

After Ruth had left, Marcy would sometimes tiptoe into her mother's closet and run her fingers down the long, silky dresses that she had chosen to leave behind. They still smelled like her perfume, musky and sweet.

*   *   *

The announcement came one Thursday at the diner, after ballet class: "I'm going to New York for the summer." Ruth sipped her water. "The bank is letting me have a sabbatical."

Marcy set down her fork. "The whole summer?"

"June through August. As soon as you're done with school."

"All by yourself?"

Ruth took a second roll from the bread bowl. "Your father and I have decided that Robert is going to come with me."

"What?" Marcy could feel the fit kicking up from her belly, moving toward her throat.

"You are going to have a wonderful time here with your father. Your last summer before junior high!"

"Why does Robert get to go?"

"You have ballet lessons. Plus your father will need the company. He still has to work. No rest for the police force." There was a lilt to this sentence, as if it was supposed to be funny.

"I can quit ballet."

"That would be a waste of money, wouldn't it? Besides, you'll never improve if you don't keep at it."

"I don't *want* to improve."

"Marcia, if I whined half as much as you when I was a child, my mother would have had me sit in the hallway of our apartment building until I came to agree with her. Can you imagine if I did that to you? My God, your father would have me arrested."

"Why can't all four of us go?"

"There are some things you cannot understand as a child," her mother said, pressing her palms flat on the plastic table. This was her stock answer for anything she didn't want to explain to Marcy, her standard indication that the conversation was over.

Marcy pushed her salad away. "I'm not hungry," she said, even though she was. An hour of ballet class always left her famished, eager to get to the plastic booth so she could devour whatever her mother was in the mood to order for them. But in searching in her head for a punishment for her mother, she could think of nothing but refusing to eat for the rest of the summer. And Ruth would have no choice but to come home and take care of her.

"Fine," Ruth said, and scooped up Marcy's croutons with a spoon. "More for me."

*   *   *

Bruce had apparently already given the summer plans all the thought he wanted to give them, because when Marcy asked him, he only sighed and said, "Yep, just you and me, kiddo," and ruffled her hair. Though her father's affection was usually enormously pleasurable for Marcy, she still felt troubled. Her father wasn't able to give her any better answer as to why Ruth was leaving. He only said, "Your mother gets her ideas, and it's best to let her follow them through. Arguing with her only makes her want to do it more."

* * *

"I think they're practicing for a divorce," Robert whispered across the dark bedroom. The nightlight flickered on the wall.

"That's not true."

"I dunno. Kelsey Sanders's parents got divorced last year, and now her sisters live in Connecticut."

"Mom and Dad love each other." Even as she said it, Marcy wasn't sure this was actually true.

"Mom says Dad's crazy to still think he's going to write a book of poetry someday."

"So?"

"So she doesn't love *everything* about him, is all I'm saying."

"What are you going to do all summer? Won't you miss everyone?"

In the dark she could see her brother's shoulders rise and fall under the covers in a shrug. "It's only for a little while. I think it might be fun."

"Not me. I wouldn't go for a million dollars," Marcy said.

He shrugged again and rolled over. After a moment, his breathing became deeper and more even. She listened to the scratch of the oak tree branches on the window.

Marcy sat up. "You're coming back, aren't you?"

"Mom says we are," Robert said, his voice thick with dreams.

* * *

They left on a three a.m. train, which meant the whole family had to wake in the middle of the night to get to the station on time. As they left town, Marcy noticed how different Lovington looked at this time of night. The moon's glow caught the edges of the lone dump truck that stood among the highway construction on the edge of town. She thought how different everything looked in the light of the moon, and she realized that this was what poetry was, as her father had explained it—seeing things in a new way. She decided to tell her father about this realization later, when they were alone.

"You'll miss the summer carnival," her father said, his eyes on the road ahead.

"Tragic," Ruth said. She was rummaging in her purse, but apparently didn't find what she was looking for, because she stopped after a moment and stared out the window.

"Send me a postcard," Marcy whispered to her brother. She had forgotten to brush her teeth, so she covered her mouth with her hand.

He looked at her. "I don't know if they have postcards in the big city," he said. Then they both started giggling, covering their mouths first and then louder, until Robert let out a whoop and Marcy followed, laughing at the top of her lungs.

"For Pete's sake, it's too early," Ruth said.

"Ruth," their father said. Then he was quiet.

At the station Marcy hugged her brother and felt a shiver of delight when he seemed as if he was going to cry. Ruth bent down and kissed her cheek. "I want to see you do a grand jeté when I come back." She straightened up and both Marcy and Robert watched as she turned to their father. "I'll call you," she said, but the words seemed to loosen something in her, and she began to cry. Their father took her in his arms and squeezed. He closed his eyes.

Marcy could feel her chest tightening, and she pulled at her mother's arm. "Who will take me to my ballet lessons?"

"Your father, of course," Ruth said. She wiped under her eyes with her thumbs and examined them for traces of mascara.

They got on the train, and when Marcy saw Robert though the window she waved her arm frantically. He made faces and pushed his cheeks out on the glass. Ruth, next to him, busied herself with becoming comfortable, wrapping a blanket around her shoulders, looking not out the window, but forward, in the direction the train pulled away and eventually disappeared.

*   *   *

The first week they were gone, her father spent most of his time in the garage, lifting weights. Marcy could hear him grunting and the metal click when he set the weights back on the rack. She had a strange energy stirring inside her, without Robert around to follow or do things with. Once she tried to go outside in her shorts and run for exercise, but she only made it down the block before a car passed and she felt foolish, like everyone in town was watching her through their windows.

Her father was gone most afternoons, driving the squad car around Lovington and filing paperwork in the office. Police work was a lot less exciting in Lovington than it was on television, he told her. Most of the time he was simply parked near the central pavilion, reading a paperback. "An occupation is just that," he would say. "A way of occupying time." When he was at work, she put on her headphones and lay on the couch with her feet on the arm, the way her mother always told her not to. Sometimes she fixed thick cheese sandwiches and ate them as she wandered from room to room, sinking her shoes into the lush carpeting.

The strangest part was not having Robert around. The two had never been separated for more than a night before, and Marcy could feel his absence somewhere in her body. There had always been a feeling of recognition when he walked into a room, as if water stopped churning and her reflection finally appeared on its still surface. Without Robert, she felt oddly exposed, as if she had been cut in half and some of her guts were showing.

* * *

Marcy's father took her to her ballet lessons, and he read a newspaper in the car instead of watching through the lobby window. Without the audience of her mother, Marcy found herself getting better. Day by day, she noticed a small improvement in the way she kept her balance and her toes turned out. Her posture improved, and once when she reached for the milk in the refrigerator she caught sight of her hand, lifting wrist first, with the fingers trailing softly after, and she marveled at how graceful it was.

In early June, the ballet teacher asked Marcy to bring her father in after class. When he came in to the studio, hulking and awkward with his paperback tucked under his arm, her teacher said, "I think

Marcy is ready to advance to her own age group. She is making remarkable progress this summer."

"I don't know. This is more of her mother's terrain." Her father picked at his mustache and blushed.

"She's not home this summer," Marcy explained.

The teacher's eyebrows lifted. "Oh? Where is she?"

"New York," Marcy said before her dad could interrupt.

"Visiting friends," her dad explained. This was news to Marcy. She fell quiet and listened.

"Well, I don't believe in letting a dancer stagnate. I think in a couple of years she'll be ready to move en pointe," the teacher said. Marcy's heart soared. She sometimes watched the advanced girls finish their class when she arrived early for hers. The wooden thumping of their toe shoes, clacking in unison as they leaped around the room, moved her deeply. She squeezed her dad's hand.

"I guess the choice is clear," her father said.

"Also, one other thing," the teacher said. "I think it's time Marcy invest in a bra."

*   *   *

A postcard from Robert arrived. On the front was a picture of the Statue of Liberty. *I ate clams at a resterant today,* the postcard read. *I thought they would be gross but they were good. Mom says PRACTICE YOUR BALLAY and say hi to Dad for us. From your awesome brother Robert.*

*   *   *

The intermediate class required black leotards instead of pink, so Marcy and her father went to the mall after the first class, which Marcy found much more enjoyable, since she was now at least the same height as the other girls. Bruce stayed out in the store, humming and flipping through a book, while Marcy went into the dressing room.

She pulled the leotard on carefully over her underwear and turned side to side in the mirror. Her body was changing so quickly she hardly recognized all the new turns and dips and hair. The black was definitely a more flattering color, casting every little roll of flesh into shadow. The bra the saleswoman at Penney's last week had picked out for her did a nice job of mashing the protrusions on her chest so they didn't even look like they were there anymore. Her father had stayed out of that part of the store, choosing instead to give Marcy the credit card while he waited on a bench by the fountain.

The saleswoman knocked. "Doing okay in there?" She poked her head in and said, "Oh, my. You look like you could be in Swan Lake any day now." Her smile showed the lipstick on her teeth.

"I might," Marcy said, flushed.

When she came out, her father was standing near the exit, talking to a man with a drooping mustache. He seemed animated, waving his arms and laughing. When he saw Marcy, he shook the man's hand and came over to the register. "That guy's a publisher for a small press in Springfield," he said, lowering his voice. Marcy felt pleased by this intimacy and leaned in. "They print poetry books," he said meaningfully, and raised his eyebrows.

"Maybe he'll publish your book, Dad!"

He smiled and tapped his credit card against the counter. "Fill 'er up," he said to the sales clerk, tipping an imaginary hat.

*   *   *

Two nights later, the publisher came over for dinner. It turned out that he was also a teacher at the local community college, and recently divorced. "Lonely," her father explained in a whisper as they spooned vegetable soup into bowls in the kitchen. When she set the food on the table, the publisher shook Marcy's hand seriously and asked that she please call him John.

John had a thin brown mustache and long, white fingers. He wore neat polo shirts and cut his meat in careful, thin strokes. He got sad at times during dinner and set down his fork as if it had become too heavy to hold.

Marcy liked him immediately. There was something about the way the air in the dining room felt when he was there, as if everything suddenly became steady. She recalled the dinners from which her mother would abruptly scoot her chair back and disappear, the way her moods could make the whole house feel as if it were vibrating.

"So your father tells me you are a ballerina," John said. "I danced myself a bit, when I was your age. My mother told my father it would help me be a better football player."

"Did it?"

"Nope," John said. He took a sip of his wine. "But I did look fabulous in a leotard."

"Ha," Marcy's father said. "Women enjoy a man in leotard. It makes them feel powerful."

"Oh, the power was all mine."

"What is it that Adrienne Rich said? 'Every journey into the past is complicated by delusions?'"

John snickered at this, his thin shoulders rising and falling. Marcy laughed a little too, but she had a feeling it was an inside joke. "To laughing often," Bruce said, raising his glass.

Later, after John had gone home and Marcy and her father were drying the dishes, she asked if John liked his poems.

"In fact, he does."

"So he'll publish your book?"

"I'm working toward that. The problem is, I don't quite have a book yet. I have the opposite of the great writer's conundrum: I have the time, but not the . . ." He waved his fingers in the air sadly. "The inspiration."

"Maybe it will come back." Marcy laid forks down carefully in the drawer. "Maybe you just need to write more. And John can come back and read it."

Her father ruffled her hair. "It's nice to have some company this summer, isn't it."

* * *

Ruth called twice a week for the first month. "Checking in," she'd say. There was a new quality about her voice, Marcy thought—it was higher, and the words more stretched out, as if she were half-singing. "How are the lessons?"

"I can go from fourth to fifth without picking my foot from the ground," she would say. "My back *développé* is the second best in the class."

"That's superb, dear," her mother would say each time. "Put Bruce on."

And Marcy would hand the phone to her father, who crossed his eyes when he said hello, making Marcy giggle. Sometimes he only talked for a couple of minutes, and other times he took the phone out to the garage, stretching the cord as far as it would go, and Marcy could hear him murmuring in a quiet voice for a very long time.

*   *   *

He began to spend longer sessions each evening in the garage gym, and when he came back in the house, flushed and smelling salty, he would have Marcy squeeze his bicep.

"Adequate?" he'd ask, wiggling his eyebrows.

"I don't think poets are supposed to have big muscles," she would answer, and her father roared with laughter. He was happier these days, laughing more easily and twirling the pencil in his fingers when he did the morning crossword. At night, she began to hear the familiar click of the typewriter again as she drifted off to sleep.

*   *   *

John began to come over more often, staying long after the dinner dishes were done, late into the night. He leaned back in his chair at the dining room table with his elbow on the table, wine class perched on his fingers, and listened to Bruce talk about his work. Then he would set his wine glass down and the conversation would drift to the economy and how difficult it was to print poetry books these days, and Bruce would refill his glass and change the subject to old movies or records they had both listened to in college.

Marcy would stay up as late as her father would allow, her eyes drooping. In her sleepy state she became aware that there was something odd about the conversation between the two men. It was as if they were talking *around* something, circling an invisible topic without directly approaching it. It was different than the conversations between her mother and father, in which sentences pointed and jabbed. With John and her father, there was a sense that the words were drawing closer and closer to one another, examining each other as if they were two lions looking one another over with curiosity.

*   *   *

In ballet, the teacher didn't stop by Marcy's place at the barre as often as she used to. Now it was like there was a magnet in the very center of Marcy's stomach, pulling the right parts in at the right times. Marcy didn't even have to think about it. She noticed it even outside of class, this feeling of being centered: when she was walking to the library, riding her bicycle, sitting on the carpet playing board games with her father and John. She could feel the string pulling at the top of her head, pulling her up straight and tightening her body.

The shorts whose elastic waist had dug into her tummy at the beginning of May relaxed their grip by the last week of June and stopped leaving lines in her skin. She was less hungry, more energetic. Some days she even forgot that her mother and Robert were gone, but then she would look at the telephone and remember with a stab in her heart that something was missing.

*   *   *

In late July, her teacher announced that they would be having a recital at the beginning of August, in the mall. Marcy told her father about it when she climbed into the car after class, still wearing her leotard. She had learned early on that her father didn't care what she wore when she got out of class.

"Recital, huh," he said. "Sounds like you're hitting the big time."

"Can John come too?"

"Sure," he said, tossing his paperback in the back seat and start-ing the car. "You can ask him yourself at dinner tonight."

"When is he going to publish your book?"

Her father sighed as he backed out of the parking space. "It's more complicated than that."

That night, when Marcy heard John mention that he had been to New York, she asked him to tell her all about it.

"It was just once. My ex-wife's friends live there." John swirled his glass. He and her father were drinking wine, and John's mouth had turned purple, his teeth almost gray.

"Was it big? And noisy?"

"I believe it was, yes. Bruce, that bread is fantastic."

"I want to go to New York," Marcy said.

"It's homemade," Bruce said. "Not too yeasty?"

"It's perfect."

"Why can't I go to New York?" She was whining, she could tell, but she couldn't stop the spark of irritation suddenly working its way through her belly.

"It's not as great as you think it is, I promise." John drained his glass.

"Still. It's not fair."

Her father nodded. His face was flushed from the wine, and his t-shirt showed off the fruits of his weight lifting. "Marsh and I kind of got the rough end of the deal, didn't we."

"We three," John said, lifting his glass to his lips, "are the col-lectors of anguish."

Bruce closed his eyes briefly, his hand pressed to his chest, a gesture Marcy had seen him make often when talking about a poem he loved. "I'm tired of hearing about New York," he said.

"So let's take our own trip," John said. "On Saturday. To Chicago."

"Really?" Marcy nearly knocked her glass over in delight.

"Really. Bruce?"

Marcy's father started to protest, but when he looked at Marcy, he said, "Why not? Why should we be the only ones who aren't having any fun?"

*   *   *

They went to the art museum downtown first. Marcy's father snapped a picture of her and John standing on the front steps. "I could lift you up so you could sit on the lion," John offered, but Marcy blushed terribly and declined, picturing him collapsing in pain under her weight. When a homeless man with a long beard that wove together like a quilt came up and asked them for money, John gave him a five-dollar bill, and Marcy thought it was so kind she had to blink to keep the tears from coming.

She bought a poster of a Degas painting for her mother and kept the tube tucked under her arm as they walked around the city in the afternoon. She tried to hold everything she saw in her mind to tell Robert later: a chocolate shop, a stroller that held three babies, a group of bicyclists with tattoos, a woman with no teeth talking about how she lost all her bus fare. All of it fell under the soft light of the evening, creating shadows that moved and fluttered so quickly Marcy became dizzy. She had to hold her hands over her ears every time the train overhead rattled by. John and Bruce would pause, midsentence, and look up at the sky as the train roared past, and when it was gone they would continue where they were, as if someone had simply placed a bookmark in the conversation.

*   *   *

For dinner, they went to a restaurant downtown with plastic green booths and low-hanging lights that cast long shadows down Bruce's and John's faces. Marcy set the poster tube next to her on the bench, next to her purse, and went to the bathroom. Her feet were starting to hurt.

She locked herself in the stall, taking care to put toilet paper on the seat the way her mother had taught her. When she pulled down her underpants, she looked down and felt as if the air had suddenly been sucked out of the stall: there, on the crotch, was a large spot of brownish blood.

She wished, suddenly and for the first time all summer, that her mother were there. Her mother would come into the bathroom and check out the underpants and pull a pad out of her purse. She pictured her mother's heart-shaped face, the stray tendrils of gray hair falling across her forehead as she bent to dig in her purse.

The bathroom door opened, a pair of heels clicking across the floor. Marcy called out. "Hello?"

The heels paused. "Yes?"

"I need something to stop the bleeding," Marcy said.

"Did you hurt yourself?"

"No."

A pause. Then: "Oh! Dear me. Is this your first time?"

"Yes," Marcy said, grateful that the woman could not see her.

"Just one minute." Marcy heard the rattling of change in a purse, a metallic crank. A manicured hand reached under the stall with a cardboard package. Marcy took it.

"Thank you," she said.

"Do you know what to do with it?"

"Yes." Marcy peeled the sticker off and placed it on the crotch of her underwear. Already she was feeling better. She listened to the woman pee and flush and wash her hands. She seemed to be hesitating around the sink after that. The clasp of a compact, the sound of a hairbrush running through hair. Then she was gone.

After dinner, Marcy asked her father for five dollars as they passed a drugstore, and he gave it to her without question. He and John were in the middle of a conversation about black-and-white movies, a subject that bored Marcy so much she couldn't even follow along. The two men stood out on the sidewalk while Marcy ran into the brightly lit store and purchased the friendliest-looking box of sanitary napkins she could find. The cashier was a teenage girl wearing too much eyeliner, and she wrapped the box in a paper bag, giving Marcy a knowing look. Her father glanced at the bag when she came out of the store, the package tucked under her arm like a football, but he didn't ask any questions. "Orson

Welles is obscenely overrated, and that's that," he said to John, and they continued walking.

They drove home late that night. As the landscape began to change around them, the interstate clearing and giving way to stretches of fields so long it felt like they were the only people on the planet, Marcy sleepily felt proud that her dad knew exactly where to go, weaving in and out of the cars around him, the other hand fiddling with the radio and waving in the air to make a point to John. At one point her eyes met his in the rearview mirror and though it was dark she could tell he was smiling.

*   *   *

Ruth called on Monday. Her voice sounded tired. "Good morning, darling, how are you?"

"We went to Chicago!" Marcy blurted out. She had visions of drawing out the story slowly, for maximum dramatic effect, but when the opportunity presented itself she found she didn't have the patience to hold it in.

"You and Dad?"

"And John. The publisher."

There was a pause. Marcy felt the low hum in her chest that meant she had done something wrong, but didn't know what it was. "We went to the art museum," she added, but her mother's silence had created a new energy on the phone, a flatness that couldn't be erased or explained.

"Put Bruce on," she said finally.

"First I want to tell you something else that happened."

"Now, Marcia. Put your father on now."

Bruce walked in from the garage in his workout clothes, mopping sweat off his forehead with a towel. Marcy dropped the phone on the table, near tears. "She wants to talk to you," she said to her dad, and fled out of the room. She began to run up the stairs, but stopped halfway and sat on the steps to listen.

Her father didn't say much at first. Just "yes" and "we did" and "all right." Then he glanced up to where Marcy sat on the steps, peering under the banister, and he walked back out to the garage.

"I know," she heard him say as he shut the door behind him, the long spiraled cord stretching across the room and under the door.

* * *

Later he came upstairs. "Good news," he said, his voice flat. "Your mom and Robert are coming home on Wednesday." He leaned against the doorframe, as if his body was too tired to hold itself up.

"I thought they weren't coming home for another two weeks."

Bruce shrugged and spread his hands out, palms up. "Your mother moves through the world on her own schedule."

"Oh." Marcy twisted her headphones in her hands. She could tell that her father was watching carefully for her reaction. "Wait," she said suddenly. "Wednesday is my recital."

"I know. We'll make it in time. This way your mom will get to be there. Don't you like that?"

"And John?"

"No, honey," he said, and turned to leave. "John is not going to be able to make it."

She listened to his soft footprints move down the stairs and into his study, where she heard the door shut and his typewriter begin clacking.

* * *

That night as Marcy lay in the dark, she had an epiphany. Her mother didn't want her father to publish his poetry book. She was jealous. In fact, her jealousy had slowly crept into the room and cast sharp shadows on the walls, lit up the posters on the wall in a green glow. As she drifted off, Marcy thought about how strange it was that a person could be in the room with you when really they were somewhere far away. It was like when her mother came in to wake her up for school—Marcy could always sense she was coming, and it jerked her awake, startling Ruth, who still stood in the doorframe, nightgown billowing.

Marcy sat up, thinking she heard a voice. She tiptoed to the door and peered out. Her father and John were walking toward the door, so she went to the window to look out.

John's car was parked out front, and the two men walked toward it gently, cautiously, almost as if they were in slow-motion in a movie. Marcy could see that there was something different about their conversation. John's shoulders were slumped, and her father put his arms around him in a hug, enveloping his thin frame the way he did when we held his children. John rested his cheek on her father's shoulder, and her father put his hand on the back of John's neck. When he leaned back, the light from the street lamp and the full moon hit his face. Marcy could see that he was crying.

Marcy felt ashamed for looking, but the twisting feeling in her gut filled her with a strange sadness, and though her father was crying, there was something about the look on his face that also made the sadness fade. He and John looked at one another, the white light of the moon creating a glow between them. They started to laugh. Marcy, alone in her room, laughed too, though she wasn't sure why.

Then they kissed.

*   *   *

It was late afternoon when Marcy and her father arrived at the train station to pick up Ruth and Robert. She stood anxiously by the track in her leotard and black skirt, leaning over to see if she could spot the train coming from the distance. Her father didn't tell her to stop. He gnawed at the skin around his thumbnail, spitting it out onto the concrete every minute or so. Once Marcy saw him press his whole hand flat against his face, fingers splayed, and she thought he might be crying again, but when he dropped his hand a moment later she could see that his eyes were dry.

She had not slept very much after seeing her father and John kiss in the yard. The next morning over breakfast she had searched her father's face for a sign that something was different now, and as she did she noticed all sorts of new details—the reddish freckle at the corner of his left eye, how thin and tall his upper teeth were. She knew that she was not allowed to ask any questions about John, or about the book, and so she kept mostly quiet for the next couple of days, trying to read, but she kept coming to the end of sentences without remembering how they had begun.

It was so bizarre, she couldn't stop her brain from remembering it over and over again, in sharp detail—the white moon on John's face, how he had wrapped his fingers around the back of her father's thick neck. Sometimes it made her stomach hurt to think of it, and other times it turned into a fantasy about John coming to pick her and her father up in his big red car, and the three of them moving to Chicago forever.

The train's long, slow horn sounded in the distance, and it arrived a minute later. Robert got off first. His face looked much different than it did at the beginning of summer—longer, with more freckles. Marcy was dismayed to see that he was wearing a shirt that she didn't recognize. His hair had grown long, the way he liked it, and it looked lighter curled over his ears. He grinned and ran into his dad's arms. Then he gave Marcy a hug, awkwardly, and to Marcy's surprise she found that she had to bend down a bit for him. She had grown, or he had shrunk.

Ruth came off the train a minute later, clutching her handbag and a suitcase. Her hair was pulled back tightly, and for a moment Marcy was startled to realize she wasn't wearing any makeup. Her face was white. She set her suitcase down and adjusted the flapping handle before leaning in to kiss Bruce. To Marcy's surprise, she kissed him on the lips, deeply. "Hello, dear," she whispered, brushing his hair back with her fingers.

Then she turned to Marcy. "You *have* lost weight," she said. She hugged Marcy's head to her chest for a long moment, pressing Marcy's face against the clanking necklaces she wore. "Look at you, look at you."

*   *   *

The car ride to the mall was quiet. Marcy had a thousand stories that wanted to spill out of her, but her mother stared out the window with a grim expression on her face and didn't seem to want to talk.

Robert fell asleep almost instantly when they got in the car, despite his excitement. "He was awake for nearly the entire train ride," Ruth said, craning her neck around to peer in the back seat. "So excited to see his father." She sighed and turned around to face the front again. "My back is so sore. I wish we could just go home."

"Marcy's been looking forward to this recital for weeks," Bruce said, his eyes flickering to the rearview mirror.

"I didn't say we wouldn't go to the recital. We're going the recital, aren't we? Don't put words in my mouth."

"I'm not."

"Trying to turn my children against me," Ruth said. She flipped down the visor and looked at her reflection in the mirror. Her eyes caught Marcy's in the mirror. "Of course we're going to your recital, honey." Ruth narrowed her eyes, and Marcy was afraid for a moment that she could see directly into her brain, to the image of her father and John outside the window. Her mother shut the visor briskly and turned her attention out the window.

* * *

The recital was held in the old drugstore in the mall, which had gone out of business and whose shelves had been stripped and moved to the walls, creating an open space full of folding chairs. The stage was a wooden platform at the back of the store. A long line of curtains was hung from old clothing racks to create a backstage. The audience was filled with parents of the dancers, based on the nervous way they picked at their hands and watched at the wiggling curtain. There were a few older people, too, with gray hair and sweaters wrapped around their shoulders, though the space was sweltering. Marcy felt hot as well and tugged at her leotard. "Where am I supposed to go?" she asked, but no one heard. Her parents and Robert had headed to the chairs to find seats together.

Marcy saw her teacher across the room and waved frantically. "You're late," her teacher said, pulling her behind the curtains, where most of the other girls from class were seated, tugging at their skirts or braiding each other's hair.

The teacher bent down and put her hands on Marcy's shoulders. "I can see you're nervous."

Until that moment, Marcy had been so focused on her parents during the car ride, and wrapped in a brief daydream that John might be at her recital, and then her disappointment that he wasn't, that she had not thought about the dancing part. But now that she pictured her mother in the crowd, watching, she felt her skin go warm. "A little, I guess."

"You don't have anything to be embarrassed about. You're a fine dancer." The teacher smiled and patted Marcy's head, then disappeared to help another girl with her shoes.

Marcy found the break between two curtains and pulled them apart just wide enough to look through. She peered out at the room, this place that used to be a drugstore. Marcy had shopped there often with her parents, waiting for their prescriptions to fill, rummaging through the toy aisle with Robert. The four of them gliding through the mall, to the parking lot, out for dinner, back home. Marcy looked around and for a moment, couldn't find them—but then she saw her father, sitting on the aisle in the third row. His legs were crossed, his thumbs tapping on his thigh nervously. She could see that he was nervous for her. Next to him sat Robert, who was frowning and leaning on Ruth's shoulder, trying to get comfortable so he could sleep. And then her mother: staring absently straight ahead of her, into the shoulder blades of the person sitting in front of her, as if she were watching a television program.

A teenage girl pressed a button on a tape player, and Marcy heard the sound of music starting. The audience applauded. Her teacher climbed atop the platform and pulled a small microphone from its stand. "Thank you all for coming," she said.

At this, the sound of the program beginning, Marcy's heart began to race. Her body seemed to understand that something was about to happen, and her breathing quickened. She looked at the other girls, who were peeking around the curtain to see their parents in the audience. Marcy took a step back.

"Watch it," hissed a beak-nosed girl.

"I don't want to do it," Marcy whispered back. She blinked away tears. A noise began to throb in her ears, a low, thundering beat. The girl's eyes were round. "You have to," she said.

The music came back on and the audience applauded once again. The teacher came back behind the curtain and clapped her hands. "Okay, girls, this is it!" A few squealed in excitement.

The girls pushed onto the stage until Marcy was the only one left standing behind the curtain. Her teacher clapped her hands again. "Come on Marcy, you'll miss your cue."

But Marcy shook her head. Her hands had gone numb, her heart was racing, and as she opened her mouth she heard it make a sticky noise, her tongue peeling from the roof of her mouth.

"You *have* to," the teacher said.

Marcy thought of her family sitting out there and she suddenly wanted to turn and run as fast as she could out the side door, across the vast parking lot, to somewhere far away, to possibly shoot up into the sky, with a great gust of wind—to be hurled into space. She felt as if there was something within her that wanted to get out, and it were pressing against her skin from the inside. She closed her eyes and covered her ears to stop the pounding sound from happening, to cover it up, and she was about to cry to drown it out, but just then the teacher put a firm hand on Marcy's back and pushed her onstage.

ANDREA UPTMOR's *writing has appeared in* Salamander, McSweeney's, Midwestern Gothic, The Chicago Reader, *and elsewhere. She has an MFA from the University of Minnesota and has been awarded the Minnesota State Arts Board Artist Initiative Grant and the Hemera Foundation's Tending Space Fellowship. She lives in Minneapolis with her wife and twin boys.*

Shrove Tuesday

Jeanne Panfely

The world, instead of ending, had covered itself in lemon trees. It was the first thing the woman noticed, in the morning, that the light from her window was blocked, or if not blocked then shaded green; trees had erupted outside, trees had erupted through her floor, and they leaned in around her bed, like a family who had been watching her sleep.

There had been warnings about this for weeks. She had seen it on the television, on a news channel—not a news channel, more like a channel that discussed the news. They had devoted, nightly, a small segment to a fringe group, a new religious movement, that now had too many followers to be ignored. The Divine Order of the Great Sixteen against the Fluoridation of Our National Waters.

Their spokeswoman had been a model in the seventies. Our woman remembered her from when she was young. The ex-model's name was Barbara Waterstern. She wore her blond hair pushed up three inches and then combed back. She had amazing cheekbones. That's what our woman thought, when she watched the not-news. What amazing cheekbones.

Barbara Waterstern's televised and talking head usually had a banner running underneath it. Something like, FLUORIDE, AN ALIEN BODY-CONTROL PLOT? And Barbara Waterstern would say something like, "Why do you think I keep coming on this show, Walter? Do you think I care what you think of me? This is beyond my life. This is beyond any of our lives. Because if the powers behind the fluoride plot are successful then the world is going to end. The human race is doomed. We're on a deadline here, Walter. Seven percent of us will be taken as slave labor. Another seven percent might be used for parts, for our organs, and our DNA. The rest of us will just be left here, on Earth, as they destroy it. Are you listening to me, Walter?"

What a cow, our woman had thought. She watched while wearing her gardening shorts and eating ice cream, mint chip. She watched while putting her bare feet up on the coffee table. A few months ago, she had broken it off with a man who hated to have feet on any surface, who had asked her to wear socks to bed. Now, she walked outside barefoot until her soles turned black. She wrapped her bare toes around the table's edge, and watched as her television program discussed Barbara Waterstern, discussed the polar ice caps, all the children who had developed asthma that year, unusual animal migrations. Some politician's sex scandal. The program put up a doomsday clock, in the bottom right of the screen, to poke fun at Barbara Waterstern and the other antifluoridians. By their calculations it was one week until the end of the world. Two days until the end of the world. Six hours. Now.

Our woman woke up on the day in question to find the world not ended. Her bedroom looked like a grove. She scooted to the edge of her bed, slipped through the tree trunks, all brand-new. "Excuse me," she said, by accident.

Her living room was covered less densely. A few saplings by the front door. The floor half-covered in patches of earth. A thick-trunked lemon tree, one that looked as though it could have been centuries old and not just a few hours, had torn through the center of her couch. Its branches spread out horizontally, were cragged and black, and pillows of yellow moss rested on them, like cotton balls.

Our woman tried to turn on the television, but the screen stayed black. The lights didn't work either. The oven clock was gone and the microwave flashed its battery-powered default. *00:00. 00:00.* Her phone was the last thing she checked. No access to the internet.

No bars to make a phone call. The trees must have pushed their roots through everything. Would she have called her son, if she had the chance? Maybe not.

She searched her house for things that worked. She laid them out, in a line, on the living room carpet. Her deceased husband's watch, still ticking. A flashlight from the garage. A solar-powered flower that danced when she placed it in the sunlight. Her alarm clock.

She put on her husband's watch. It was nine fifteen a.m. Losing track of time seemed like the surest way to lose track of everything.

Our woman expected to find chaos in the streets, or at least people, or at least the streets, but all she could see were the lemon trees. All the negative space of the world had been filled in. It felt like our woman had been walking down the stairs and miscalculated the number of steps, a sudden shift in worldview. It took her a moment to adjust, standing on her front stoop, and she searched for what had once been her lawn, and beyond that the road, and beyond that a neighbor's house, but the closest she came to seeing any of it was in the remains of her paved walkway. Pierced by the trees that had grown through it, it was now reduced to gravel. And her car, in the space that was once her driveway, impaled by so many trees that must have kept on growing, was now hovering a few feet off the ground.

Our woman wondered if this was some sort of attack, a strange kind of warfare. It seemed unlikely. The trees looked inviting, bushy things, and full of yellow fruit. Our woman wanted to walk through them, and anyway what did she have at home, to stay and protect? She wanted to leave, but she didn't want to get lost. She went back inside, rifled through the closet where she had hidden most of her husband's old things. The things she hadn't gotten rid of. His old ties and the bird houses he used to build and the little wooden clowns he had once made for their son, one standing upright holding a balloon supported by wire, one balancing on his little clown head. Her husband had painted them himself. They weren't what she was looking for and she put them aside, stood them up, on the floor outside the closet.

The thing she was looking for was a heavy old case, filled with poker chips, reds and whites and greens. She dumped them all into her largest purse. She slung the purse over her shoulder. She picked up the flashlight and then she glanced at her phone. She scrolled through all of the numbers, all of the people she couldn't call. She tossed it onto the floor. It felt thrilling to leave it behind, thrilling to reduce the object to its parts, just metal and plastic. Our woman headed out, dropping poker chips behind her as she weaved through the trees. The sequence from her front door went red, red, white, red, green, green.

She wondered what Barbara Waterstern was doing now. It felt strange to think she might never again see that face on TV again. Our woman remembered an exercise tape Barbara had put out in her prime. Our woman's mother had bought it. Barbara in a leotard, high crested over her thighs. Leg warmers. And kick, and kick, and kick, and breathe. Our woman's mother imitated it in their living room.

Our woman started picking the best lemons. She put them in her purse, let them roll around over the poker chips. But really, all the lemons were the best lemons. She had never seen anything like them. Nothing had ever been so yellow and so full.

Our woman thought about what she could do with them. Her mother used to make lemon bars, lemon bars dusted with powdered sugar. No ovens, our woman reminded herself.

The heat was crushing. Our woman tried knocking on a few houses but no one answered. Our woman peered through windows. "Hello?" she called. She could only see more trees.

One person was home, standing on the other side of a locked front door, but he called at her to go away. Everyone was frightened of the trees. "They aren't so bad!" our woman called back. "The trees are fine!" But there was just silence on the other side and after that, she stopped knocking on doors.

Our woman walked for miles. Her bag was now missing half of its poker chips, the other half a trail behind her. She wished she had a map of the town, or even just a compass. She could see shades of buildings through the trees, but they all looked the same. Eventually, she found a group of people, dressed like firefighters. They had on gas masks. They were standing around one tree, a large one, holding axes out in front of themselves, tentatively. They hadn't hit it, not yet. One man, a young man, lifted up his mask as she passed. "Don't touch the trees!" he called out to her. "We don't know what they want!"

The woman smiled but said nothing as she passed them by. She palmed a lemon in her purse. She held her hand out to a tree, dragged her fingers across rough, lemon bark. The part of her life that had involved men telling her what to do had ended a long time ago.

Eventually, she found a building that was not a house. The old movie theater. The theater that was always about to be shut down, always fundraising to be saved. Before the lemon trees, women used to stand outside with clipboards, asking our woman for money. *The Lark Theater is a town landmark, don't you want to help save it?* The first time this happened, our woman donated twenty dollars. Every time afterward, she made sure to cross the street.

There were four movie posters outside. The theater always chose the worst movies. A romantic comedy from the eighties. A French film our woman hadn't heard of. Two poster slots were filled by requests for donations. *Save The Lark Theater! Donate Now!*

The glass door leading into the lobby was smashed. Our woman couldn't tell if this had been the work of looters or trees. Our woman crossed through it, into the lobby. This theater had the worst popcorn too. No butter and no salt. Always stale. And there it is, that's why, our woman thought. The machine still filled with yesterday's popcorn. They probably would have sold it again today.

She crossed the lobby into the theater room. There was only one room here, at this theater. The room was completely dark and she flicked on the flashlight. She walked to the emergency exits and propped them all open, two in the front and two in the back. This gave the room a slight glow.

The trees had broken through here too. One in the fifth row, one in the eighth row, two in the back, like teenagers, leaning into each other, on a date. Our woman chose a spot near the middle. She checked the time. It was nearly noon.

She put her purse onto her knees and looked inside. Lemons and poker chips. Our woman had once had a boyfriend, in college, who would peel lemons, peel them and eat them whole. It was everything about the senses. He'd drip lemon juice down his chin. He'd spit seeds into the sink. He'd kiss our woman, and even now that's what kisses tasted like to her, echoes of lemon juice.

Our woman thought of everything she knew about lemons. Hadn't they once protected sailors against scurvy. Couldn't they be used for cleaning. Couldn't they be used for preservation. Lemons to stop apples from turning brown. Lemons to save bananas. Our woman wondered if the whole world might last a little longer now, lemons saving everything. Lemons cleaning the whole world and stopping it from becoming something else. Something else like what it had been recently; sickly sweet and rotting away.

Our woman dug her nail into the skin of one of the lemons. The best one, the most yellow. She pulled back the rind from the flesh, and it spit at her, misted. She peeled it all the way. It looked so strange without its peel, wrong, like an orange that got sick, or wasn't fully ripe. It looked like a baby's fist. It was nearly glowing in this half light, a room meant for darkness, now filled with midday sun. She decided she understood the Fluoride Plot. It had been an act of kindness. Strengthening everyone's teeth so they could all indulge in lemons, when the lemons came. That wasn't right. She put the whole lemon into her mouth anyway, chewed it, swallowed it seeds and all. She kept going. She wanted to think of nothing but lemons. She wanted her mouth to go numb from the acidity. She wanted to eat all the lemons in the world.

JEANNE PANFELY is a fiction writer from Marin County, California. She received her M.A. in Creative Writing from the University of California, Davis. Her work has been presented in Litro Magazine *and through Stories on Stage, Davis. She was the recipient of the Walter and Nancy Kidd Prize. She currently lives in Portland, Oregon, where she is working on her first novel.*

Questions
for Anesthesiologists

Robert Glick

1. Why have you become available only now?
Because we're diversionary with our obliterations. Because the grief
of others renders you invisible, even to yourself.

2. How would you explain anesthesiology to beginners?
Through the application of anesthetics, we attempt to lessen bodily
pain during and after surgery.

3. How long have humans used anesthetics?
We roll in mud, we suck on specific grubs, we stand for the seventh-
inning stretch.

4. When did you decide to become an anesthesiologist?
Many early magics pushed me there.

I came home from the orange groves near the power plant,
where me and my friends, the Girl Moriarties, we dared each other
to touch the moldy ones, globes gone soft, the ones gone churlish
and iridescent green. We were ten, eleven, hurling the most pliable

against tree trunks, in love with their circulatory system of citrus gushing onto the summer dirt.

I unlocked the door to my house. I was sweaty, my forehead sap sticky. My grandfather sat in Dad's recliner, smoking his pipe, which he wasn't supposed to smoke, on account of preemphysema. The entryway smelled like vanilla tobacco. His USS *Nimitz* cap, slightly tilted.

"Your grandma's at the market getting you some Slim Jims," he said. And then he told me that my parents had disappeared. No trace, no note.

"But their cars are here," I said.

"The police are looking," he said. "They're eagle eyed."

So the first magic was the certainty that my parents' homecoming was marionetted not to the police, but to my ingenuity and will.

Then the daily magic of arcane bargains.

The penultimate magic, nine months later, when I pressed the chloroform-soaked cloth to my grandma's face.

And the most potent magic a week after that, when my parents actually returned.

5. Are you suggesting that anesthesia is a kind of magic?
We know anesthesia works: we don't always know how, or why. So we put our ears to the ground. The black box of caudal blocks, the parsing of oscilloscope waves and bell parabolas. Pulse oximetry, core temp. Cut open, gauge effects, stitch shut. And though we can't see the gas permeating the brain-blood barrier and pinching down the neurons, it does its job, indifferent to whether we call it science or magic.

If you let it, anesthesia is a kind of magic, because magic engenders plenitude. But I already felt complete, or completed. I had the baby inside me. I would come home, exhausted from surgery, and my husband Chuck would giddily do this balance beam walk on the top edge of the couch. He'd ask what type of bean the baby had multiplied into since this morning, and I'd say plum bean or gumball bean, and my teenage children, Russ and Jess, would be fighting across the dinner table about whether we should buy cloth or synthetic diapers.

Keep your hands to yourself, I kept telling everyone.

"Do you want the diapers to hug," Jess asked, "or do you want them to pamp?"

6. How safe is anesthesia?
The United States, in 2015: under supervised conditions, human error notwithstanding, monstrously safe.

7. Then what happened to the cartographer?
We were a few hours into a liver transplant. I was telling Minh, the anesthesia resident, about how my friend Lacey, an OBGYN, had a map of Orcas Island in her office. She had a summer home there, off the coast of Washington State. I wanted to ask the cartographer about how they developed their nautical maps, the curves of sounds and currents that reminded me of the moving shapes of fogs.

"That's a little weird," Minh said.

Moreland, the surgeon, started talking about his "old man knuckles." I noticed a jagged crack in the soap dispenser, as if it had been dropped. And then some invisible error crept in. The beeping, and the machines graphing out their zeroes, and the EKG's flattened seismograph.

8. What did you do to keep the cartographer alive?
I had never seen a case fall apart so quickly. I looked at the cartographer's liver scooped from its shell. My face started shaking. I felt the weight of several leaden blankets draped heavy over my shoulders.

9. Why do you keep your wedding ring pinned to your bra?
Last year, I had left it in the pocket of my scrubs, had an impossible time retrieving it from the hospital laundry chute. After that, Dr. Watermelon (that's what Russell calls himself) had

written on the white board in my office: ___ *Days Without a Ring Accident.*

Eventually I ran out of lemon yellow Post-its. From then on, every day was day ninety-six.

In the locker room, I unpinned the ring from my bra, pushed it back onto my finger. Some warble code blurted through the intercom. What had happened? Something with the airway, but what? What did we do wrong?

10. Did you want to speak with the cartographer's wife?

Not at first.

Lacey harbored an intense dislike for Moreland. As with most surgeons, he lugged his imperious anvil of testosterone, necessary in the operating room, out into the unsterile world.

I didn't appreciate his refusal to share his SodaStream sparkling lime water. Yet he was an excellent surgeon, and he didn't always ask about the baby.

He was clearly too blunt, too diagnostic to talk to the cartographer's wife.

So I got my ass off the locker-room bench. I raked my forearms with my nails. I brushed my teeth, swished the stinging mouthwash, and walked to the waiting room.

When I saw her through the porthole, the brain in its soft box went blank. I watched her reading a *Better Homes and Gardens*, or not really reading, tracing the wings of the bird that provided the frame for whatever puff piece.

Then all the guilt rushed up. Here I was with the baby and she had no idea that she was in the process of losing and before the cartographer went under, he didn't know either, didn't know that he wouldn't come up.

How badly I wanted to hold my hand up to hers, this circle of thick, scratched glass between us, to make a steeple of our fingers! She had these beautiful freckles on her cheeks, and kept making and unmaking a fist, as if arthritic. I wanted to apologize for everything: his death, the astronomical odds of it, the fake roses in the fluted vase by her elbow.

A woman approached. The tips of her clacking heels were candy-apple red. Something about her mouth seemed intelligent and lost.

"We can't let you go in there," she said. She was from legal.

"Are we so inhumane that I can't console a woman who has just lost her husband?"

"Every word you say to her can be refracted one thousand ways that suggest our fault."

"It probably was our fault!"

The cartographer's wife must have heard us arguing; she looked at us through the porthole. I saw her using the serrated edge of a candy-bar wrapper to get something out from under her nail. I remembered some animation on the internet, something Jess had shown me, where a woman's freckles turned into brambling finches.

"We don't know anything yet," the woman said. "Now please, come with me. We have some questions."

I held up my hand to the cartographer's wife, who may or may not have seen me, and I let myself be hooked away.

11. What questions?

I can only tell you that there was a piece of macaroni salad on the conference table, repulsively viscous with mayo, until the woman napkinned it up. I can tell you *yes* or *no*, *yes* or *no*. And that the numb sadness I had felt at the cartographer's death became a desiccating rage.

12. What did Lacey give you?

A crystal, of all things.

I paged Moreland; he didn't call me back. Can you believe he still insisted on a pager?

I exhausted myself walking up the six flights of stairs to my office. The echo of my Crocs *slap slap* past the upside-down stencil of Obama's face, *epoh* scratched into the gunmetal grey paint below the emergency-exit sign. I took off my shoes and opened the bottom drawer of my desk. Usually I liked the rustle of the papers against my stockings; now the air in the drawer felt rancid and torpid to my feet.

I must have missed something. I would accept whatever watery morass of consequences got flung my way.

Lacey came in; she must have heard. "Take this," she said, handing me the crystal.

"What is this shit? This woo shit?" The slang, I had learned it from Jess. Lacey knew that I despised objects that held no intrinsic power other than what you invested in them. Symbolic vaginas, she would call them, except she considered it a positive.

"Use it, don't use it," she said. "Cover your mirror. Do a death ritual, any one will do."

I set the crystal against the tangly roots of my orchid, which I suspected was sick with scale.

"Sit with me," I said.

Together we watched the traffic. I moved over to the windowsill, let my index finger squish in and off the tip of a cactus spine. Someone sped by in a convertible. It felt strange to see the top of their head from this angle, as if one could drop down a line, ice fishing for a snapshot of the brain, what driving and braking and turning did to the synapses, some extraneous thought about a piñata that never broke at a birthday party.

13. After Lacey went to her episiotomy, you still didn't go home?

I loved my family, and of course I loved the baby, but everything at home was the baby: appointments and preparations and speculations. Would it weigh more or less than Dr. Watermelon? Which second language should it master? What if it turned into a Republican?

So instead I gazed at the crystal. Could it heal the scale? Could it be sacred in any way? Did the crystal have actual healing properties, something unmeasurable by science? Something about its symmetric molecular structure? Or did the crystal fake me into paying more attention to the orchid? Did it get me to water it more regularly? To apply the rubbing alcohol? Miracle-Gro? What if the physical proximity of the crystal, the way it leaned against the stem, provoked some kind of reactive response that repelled the scale?

What if the bugs just got bored of being there? What if the orchid pitied me? Why did I purchase something so un-self-sufficient? What if the diffuse consciousness of the orchid was doing me a favor, repelling the insects not from its own self-preservation, but to rectify for me what had become unbalanced in me by the baby, which asked me to ignore the magic of gases, which might have contributed to the cartographer's death?

14. How did you handle the family that night?
I tried to be a quiet, translucent version of myself. I tried to appreciate the small gestures by which my husband showed his love. Tonight he had put the chicken in the oven at the correct time, and had remembered to wrap the tin foil over the edges of the broiler pan, to prevent extra mess and heat loss.

At the dining-room table, Jess and Russ were pontificating on dumb questions, like if Pluto wasn't a planet any more, was plutonium no longer radioactive? Jess told me that wishbones were stupid and I agreed, and she didn't like that I agreed, so then wishbones were now the bomb, even better than tuning forks.

Russ started juggling oranges. He dropped one, which rolled under the table, and, spurting out his teen chemicals, he banged his head standing back up.

"I thought we'd be able to wait for the baby," Chuck said to him, "to put felt on all the sharp corners."

"Very funny," said Russ, rubbing his head. "That actually hurt."

I kept trying to imagine the cartographer's dining room, but I couldn't: it was scaffolding, an empty set. I excused myself and went upstairs.

15. Did you finally say something to Chuck?
I was half-asleep, an eye mask over my face. Chuck brought in some paint swatches for the guest room, which we had decided to convert into the nursery. I had never enjoyed that room. Something about the ivy in the wallpaper border, and how the room had those older, two-prong electrical outlets, which made me think that I'd have to go pee in the outhouse.

"The challenge," Chuck said, "is to find a color that can accommodate either a boy or a girl."

"Can we talk about it tomorrow? I'm beyond beat. And besides, we'll find out soon enough."

"It's not that. I'd like to do something not blue or pink." He bent over, held up each swatch to the night-light by his ankle. "Are you tired from the baby?"

"Not the baby," I said. That's when I explained the cartographer's death, that Moreland and I would have to make a presentation to our colleagues.

"Moreland's the guy who flies his own Cessna?"

"Yeah."

"Sorry," he said. "That's some added stress."

As if worse for me than for the dead cartographer.

"Would you like anything?" he asked.

"Can you soak my eye mask in lavender?"

"I meant anything within reason." He kissed me, smacked a kiss on my belly, and went downstairs to watch his Royals, his highlights, his replays.

16. Why did Chuck want this baby so badly?

We hadn't planned it.

Three years ago, we had actively decided against it.

At my urging, we had even forged a list of how, in the absence of a third child, we would embrace our middle age. Sitting up in bed watching jazz documentaries not by Ken Burns, purchasing season tickets one section below the nosebleeds, relishing the vicarious pleasures exuded by children in their various adult stages.

I wanted to publish a paper in the *Journal of Clinical Anesthesia*; Chuck started talking about buying the jewelry store from Mr. K.

Once we found out, however, Chuck made the baby Copernican, a pole star. Why? Maybe he missed taking care of Russ and Jess in their presentient incarnations. I think he viewed the baby as a miracle, bucking the near impossibility of statistics—for me to get pregnant, at my age, with the IUD inside me.

With my glass eye, I admit, I felt happy enough with our future. Yet the pregnancy seemed like a tectonic shift, as irreversible as time or mold. I couldn't ignore this magic, or the ferocity of Chuck's wanting. To refuse it invited hex-level consequences. Maybe, after so many years, we required and deserved new, novel forms of joy. So I said *yes*, and Chuck danced around the house with his stepladder, vacuuming out cobwebs from the corners of ceilings, and I let myself imagine the baby squeezing the air from Sophie the rubber giraffe.

17. What did you do with all the paint swatches?

After my parents disappeared, I played endless games of tetherball; the insides of my wrists were always inflamed. An early supper, my grandma making green beans topped with parmesan cheese, and then best-of-three at Connect Four with my grandpa. I sat on the oval rug. He sat in his recliner, directing me where to put his pieces.

After, I went to my room to draw another maze.

I did not draw a labyrinth, with minotaurs and maidens and Theseus with his rusty sword. I drew the maze after Daedalus got imprisoned, how the erasure of the architect made the space unmappable.

On the back of each maze, I wrote a new story about my parents.

Hacking at corpse flowers somewhere in Borneo.

Posing as Mormon missionaries in Uganda, infiltrating the illegal sapphire trade.

Russian spies, an operation called The Mantle, a wintry operation in the tunnels of the Novolazarevskaya Station.

Always alive, always deep in intrigue, always able to explain why they had to leave so quickly, why Grandma couldn't tell me where they had gone.

And so the magic dust to stabilize my parents' impossibilities got sprinkled onto the maze, lighting up the invisible patterns to their whereabouts.

Now, on the bedspread, unable to sleep, I laid out the swatches, made a maze of the lighter greens, and I let everything that could have possibly killed the cartographer orbit around me. Pale star, artichoke heart, Denver grass. As if anything was within reason. As if reason was a box or a maze, which was usually square, sometimes circular or triangular, but rarely in the shape of a bird.

18. You paged Moreland again?

I needed something that I knew he couldn't give me: a reminder that the cartographer's death was ours to bear.

"You have to accept that it happens," he said, "and move on."

"I know it happens! But what went wrong? Something went wrong."

"Nothing that we did."

"How can you be so sure?"

"I'm sure."

I felt sorry for him. The pink collared shirts, the smell of his antibacterial skin. I hoped that somewhere in his house, in a secret room hidden under a throw rug, he had sequestered his heart in a box. Maybe, at the occasional safe times, he would take it out and stroke its fur.

"We have to make sense of it!" I said.

"Let's talk about it once a grand rounds date is set."

"Do you feel bad at all?"

"Unlike you," he said, "I can separate sadness from guilt."

"You're a robot," I said, and hung up.

19. Yet you followed his lead?

With my glass eye, I used to say to my parents, often while chewing a pinky nail, I have to admit that I cheated on the question about Sherman's march to the sea.

With my glass eye, I have to admit that I didn't like grandma's stench all along the sofa.

With my glass eye, I have to admit that over the next week, I let the baby's needs take over, let myself be reconfigured. My swelling, my hungers. The cartographer's death became a little less real, a little more abstract. The intricacies of the case slipped away.

I let the baby do its job, pulling softly on its nutrients, until the miscarriage undid.

20. If you feel comfortable with it, can you tell us what happened?

Biology happened. The magic which we call bad luck or bad wiring, that happened.

I had done an early surgery, a knee replacement. At home, Jess and I, at the kitchen table. A lazy afternoon, a rare peaceful moment between us. Two men on the radio debated the racially motivated ethics of gerrymandering, something about cracking and packing, which I mostly ignored. I cut celery sticks; Jess filled the canoe part with peanut butter.

I asked her if she remembered dressing up as Louis Pasteur, maybe fifth grade, for a speech contest.

"I should have been Marie Curie," she said.

"Why? You're still obsessed with Pasteur."

For many years, since the rabid-dog incident, she celebrated July 6, the administration of the first rabies vaccine, in place of her own birthday. I'd take her to the gag store, where she'd buy rubber bats.

"I guess," she said. She licked the peanut butter off the knife. "It was fourth grade, because I didn't get my braces yet."

"You remember how the fake beard kept tilting?"

"It was soooo mortifying." She made a guttural noise, something between spit and explosion, and stomped upstairs to change into her cross-country gear. I took the tape measure that Chuck had left on the sink and pulled out its tongue and let it retract; I liked the sound. I chomped on a piece of celery, felt the peanut butter stick to the roof of my mouth. The odd vulnerabilities of cats, I thought, at which point the pain hit me and I doubled up in the chair, felt wet in my underwear. I didn't look. I knew, though I didn't know how bad.

I screamed Jess back downstairs.

"What did I do now?" she asked, came down grumbling, then saw.

21. Which hospital did you go to?

I wouldn't let Jess drive me to my hospital.

22. Was the baby already gone?

Jess walked me to the admissions desk and ran out through the ambulance dock.

Chuck got there an hour later, heard that I had lost the baby, and punched someone's cluster of Mylar balloons.

Once they released me, we found Jess lying in the back of the minivan, her sneakers pressed against the tinted glass.

23. What did you do to grieve?

I kept my hands over my belly. I watched the light shift through the bedroom shutters.

The house smelled like cracked pepper.

Dr. Watermelon taught himself how to use the blender, to make protein shakes. He wore headphones everywhere and didn't hear the grinding.

I asked him weakly, through the Percocet, to take off the headphones, because the lowercase *b* on the ears made me think of Beatrice, my secret name for her.

I imagined myself sitting in a folding chair at her high school-graduation. How old I'd be, almost fifty-eight, and how I would smooth my skirt, and how the cucumber magnolias would be in bloom.

I felt my evolution curtailing, the edemic water receding from my toes, the itchy ache of each stitch, and I let the emptying burrow in.

24. Why did you keep her name to yourself?

Except for Chuck, who had magneted a list of names to the extra fridge in the garage, we all had secret names for her. Jess referred to her, in retrospect, as Thing 3. My son confessed that he called her Sprocket, adding a gear to our machinery.

25. Why do you dislike television shows about plane crashes?

The night of the miscarriage, Dr. Watermelon went out and came home, chattering about flops and rivers.

I asked Jess to fetch me a staple remover.

"Get it yourself," she said. "Doesn't your chart say that you're as healthy as a horse?"

Everyone seeping out a surfeit of themselves.

The night after, I came downstairs to microwave a hot pack, and to ask Chuck to put earthquake latches on the armoire drawers. We weren't due for another three hundred years, based on data from the New Madrid quakes of 1812. Still, I wanted the smell of wood glue; I wanted the extraordinary sense of smell that pregnancy didn't produce.

Chuck wiped his face with his beer, camouflaging tears with condensation.

"Come sit with me," he said. He was binge-watching a show about plane crashes. I heard engines sputtering, the explosive breach of a metallic hull.

"I hate these shows," I said.

"Just one?" he asked. "It's set in Peru."

"You see that seagull picking at a potato-chip bag by the memorial on the beach? It's not beautiful!"

"Sorry!" he said. "I only wanted a snuggle."

The microwave dinged. I wrapped the hot pack in a dish towel. I saw a cockpit filling with smoke.

26. What got you thinking about the cartographer again?

I couldn't stand this link between psychological closure and the solution of complex problems. How survivors and relatives of the deceased, to prevent other lost lives, forced their way past bean counters, circumvented the involutions of regulatory bodies, excavated the hidden flaws in maintenance processes and design documents.

I thought I didn't want to hear how everything could be explained away. But that's exactly what I wanted: to turn the inexplicability of magic back into science. So I opened my computer and watched the tape of the cartographer. Black-and-white, without sound, the cartographer about to die, and dying, with you and your straw-like hair sticking out from under the cap, flailing about the dials.

My lungs felt flattened. I took short, thin breaths.

Okay, Grace, I said to myself, how could I give the cartographer's ghost a voice box, so that he could tell us what we needed to know?

27. You reject Lacey's woo, and yet: ghost, magic, maze?
Ghosts, I was certain, lived in the data. Airway readouts, preoperative surveys, a photo I found while skimming his online obituary: the cartographer and his wife on a half-broken swing, one of her royal blue pumps dangling off his foot.

28. Regarding the case, what specific data did you look at?
It was late the next night. A diminishing, irregular cramping in my uterus. Me in the bedroom, reading about the vasodilator effects of isoflurane on the hepatic circulation.

I heard Chuck coming up the stairs. Impulsively I ran into the bathroom, book in hand, and closed the door. I wasn't mad at him; I just didn't want to hear about his needs. My suffering, I imagined, was a bowl filled with water, and his feelings were another bowl floating on top, making my water overflow.

Chuck opened the door. He was sweating, a line of drops above his brow; most likely he and Russ had been lifting weights. He wore loose green shorts from his high school, with the white animal decal, a tiger or cougar, mostly peeled off.

"You're not using the bathroom in a conventional manner," he said.

I realized the toilet seat was down. I started to cry.

"What is it?" he asked.

I closed the door on him.

29. What did Moreland's daughter have to do with Jess?
I kept trying to get Moreland to help me figure out the cartographer's death. During one surgery, I said: "Have we looked at hepatocellular integrity?"

"Barely relevant," he said. Usually he'd just say *no*, without explanation. His mouth, like an urban planner designing a street grid made only of cul-de-sacs. I resented and admired his self-confidence.

His teenage daughter was becoming more difficult, he told the resident. She worshipped some band named Slayer.

"She's still got a soft center," he said, "despite the jean shorts and the cherry lipstick."

I thought about Jess. Most nights since the miscarriage, she went up to the treehouse, doing her homework until after midnight, a row of patio cushions for a mattress.

Moreland had even bought a Slayer album, one called *Seasons in the Abyss*, to try to understand. "I nearly choked on my wine," he said. "It sounded like the copulation of a garbage compactor and a boiling lobster. Mosquito forceps, please."

To bond with her, he invoked the music's rage, its darkness. She responded by telling him that he was shittier than an oil stain at a monster truck show. A waste of bile.

"The point," he said to us, "is that at some primate level, she noticed me putting in the time. And that will help us down the road."

"Gah," I said.

"You disagree?" he asked.

"Not exactly," I said.

30. You didn't confide in your husband, yet you tried to reconcile with Jess?

No one talked to me, after my parents were gone, or after they returned.

Someone should have said, What do you need? Should have said, I'll be an ear, an openness, a waiting room.

I spent entire afternoons under the crackle of power lines, torturing fallen oranges. I starved myself except for Grandma's green beans and Hostess cherry pies and root beer. On the gopher-divoted track I sprinted until I stumbled hard, my knees always raw and scabby, and the boys gathered in the bleachers, betting on how many laps I'd run before I'd collapse into the long jump pit.

Someone should have talked to Jess, years ago, after the rabid dog, before she became the little scorpion.

Yes, I should have said, that must have been so terrifying.

31. What did you say to her?

I eavesdropped; her new friend Lix was on speakerphone. Something about n minus minus meaning n minus one, and problems with GitHub commits.

I knocked on the door and came in. I heard Lix say, "You stupid git!" And my daughter laughing flirtatiously.

"Hang on," Jess said to Lix. She held the phone at her side, staring at me. "It's my Mom, dragging herself into my personal space."

"Can we talk?" I asked.

I could only imagine, I said, how hard it must have been, a fourteen-year-old, without even a learner's permit, having to drive me to the hospital, to bear my whimpering, the blood on the floor mat.

"You can always talk to me," I said.

"Why would I want to?"

"You don't have anything you want to tell me? Or ask me?"

"Yeah," she said. "Can I go to the corn maze with Lix on Wednesday night?"

Putting in the time, I told myself.

"I'll have your dad drive you," I said.

32. Did you not see the connection between your mazes and the corn maze?

I was too busy worrying about Jess, who couldn't see past her anger, and feeling rotten that I had nothing to offer.

If you had asked me why I made mazes, I'd answer, maybe to be two people? To be at once wandering inside the corn maze and on the metal bridge above, getting my bearings. To be at the same time the architect Daedalus, who made the maze, who saw with the raven's eye, and the hero Theseus, who, at ground level, solved it.

33. How far is it from Kansas City to Phoenix?

5,538,720 feet, said my husband.

Chuck's only uncle, Mort, had passed away. On top of everything else.

It pained him to leave me, Chuck said, pain as deep as the deepest trench, the kind with glow-in-the-dark squid, but would I mind if he went to the funeral this weekend?

Chuck considered himself intimately bonded to his uncle, a selfish and generous man, a man nicknamed "Old Faithful" for the way he periodically lost track of his pressure gauge, and whom, we suspected, picked bar fights well into his sixties. Mort, according to Chuck, had given him The Reckless, which caused Chuck to perform stupid acts in times of stress.

"I don't mind," I said. "Not a bit."

"Great. I'll start digging through Travelocity."

I went back to the bedroom, enraged that he took my agreement at face value. I googled *Jewish cover death mirror*. I found a sheet—the most somber we had, the color of brown M&M's—and flung it over the wall mirror.

That hurt my abdominal muscles.

"It's doing that thing again!" Chuck yelled. Our computer must have glitched again into pixelated chevrons. He called to Jess for tech support.

The sheet pleased me. Now I couldn't see my bloodshot eyes, how my body was returning to form.

34. Why didn't Chuck take the mirror seriously?

"Jewish people do it," I told him. "A way of mourning the baby." How the Jews considered it important not to adorn the self during grieving. Also, the more Lacey-like closing of the mirror's demon gateways, to prevent negative energy from seeping in at this vulnerable time.

"For how long?" he asked.

"For as long as it takes!"

"Wow, I meant the Jews. How long do they keep up the sheet?"

"Oh. Seven days, usually."

"Jeez, Grace. If you don't want me to go, say so!"

"I really will be fine," I said.

"Why do you make me seem so extraneous?" he asked. "Jess wants to go to Phoenix with me. She doesn't think I'm extraneous."

"You're not extraneous!" I said. "I'll have Dr. Watermelon on call."

Sometimes Chuck would pretend to comb his hair in the covered mirror. I wasn't sure if he was belittling me or if he were looking at some spectral version of himself. Its presence, I suspect, offended him: its continual insistence that nothing, not even the three hours he spent shredding out-of-date tax returns, would make the miscarriage even close to okay.

35. Things kept getting worse?

There were moments of normality. Me and Chuck were talking about Russell's chemistry teacher, who had given Russell an article about film processing and skin color. But then Chuck would say something like, "When can we have sex again?" and I could almost feel a thickness of bubble wrap settling around my heart.

"Back off!" I said. 'It's too soon! Too soon to even think about."

And then Chuck left to pick up Jess and Lix at the corn maze and no one came back.

36. What did you do?

After calling Chuck the first time, the second time, the third time? After texting him hearts, because I felt guilty about my moods? After I couldn't even read past the abstract of a study on transesophageal echocardiography? After Jess didn't answer her phone either?

Russell was home because he was on restriction. Every night since the miscarriage, he had found a delicate way to break his curfew. Once, he had lost track of time trying to scrape pigeon poop off the windshield. Another night, a contest with friends over the fastest poker chip-flip.

"Should we the call the cops?" I asked him.

"Chill," he said.

I grew feral with worry. I listened to the frenetics of Ornette Coleman. I went through the week of unopened mail: KCP&L bill, Planned Parenthood, *Lapidary Journal*.

I didn't pour myself a drink, because alcohol was an admission of the worst.

If Chuck or Jess was dead, would we stay in this house? This city?

I turned on the downstairs television. It was equally my fault that *Girls Gone Wild!* was playing on every single cable channel. Some bikini climbing the ladder to the lifeguard tower. The way water beaded on the skin of breasts.

Finally I got a text from Jess. She was hanging out at Lix's house. *Where is your father?* I texted.

NO KLUE, she wrote.

I hated him, even if he had been mauled by bears. I texted once more. It was four seventeen a.m. *Please*, I said, *just write back.*

37. Chuck's disappearance triggered memories of your parents?

Not my parents. My grandparents.

Every day, my grandpa gave me scratchy hugs. He washed the utensils, handing them to me to towel-dry, telling me stories about his tour on an aircraft carrier. The mop duty, the dice games in stairwells.

Under the pretense of my own maturation, my grandma avoided me. I made my own salami-and-cheddar sandwiches, folded my own shirts.

My grandma knew something, I was sure. When I'd ask her, she'd wrinkle her nose. I started to hate her for so obviously lying to me, for the lonely expanse of my freedoms.

I stole her keys, checked her glove compartment for envelopes franked with foreign stamps.

Often I fell asleep under the piano until my grandmother shook me awake. I hated her for that as well, for dragging me back into this waking world, a world where successfully exiting one night's maze simply led to the maw of the next, the electric clock in your bedroom flicking its numbers over the edge.

38. What did you do when Chuck came home the next morning?

I cried, I was that angry. And of course I was relieved. And guilty, when I saw his cheek swollen purple, the bruise shaped like the bulbous end of a bone, and he was dragging one leg behind him, and his hair, the color of Golden Grahams, all frizzed out.

He had gotten in a crash, he told me. He had no means of contacting me and he was so unbelievably sorry.

That's all he would say.

I should have gotten him an ice pack, a slab of meat for his cheek; I didn't. He sat on the couch, holding the edge of his belt. He seemed sad and old. He slowly balled up one sock, flung it onto the coffee table.

"You really have nothing to explain?" I asked.

"I can't."

"Is there something you think I can't handle?"

"Something I need to handle myself."

"You're an ass," I said. "A real ass. I'm going upstairs."

"Why?"

"You said you have nothing to say, and I have three surgeries tomorrow. Three. You know what? You can sleep in the fucking nursery!"

I was glad that wounded him.

"I'm keeping quiet for you," he said.

"Are you?"

"I am," he said. "You can't see it yet." I watched him limp to the kitchen, where he got a Gatorade, which he pressed to his forehead. His other sock, an old Christmas present, a Dr. Seuss Grinch sock, still on his foot. I went upstairs to sleep.

39. What couldn't you see?

A maze possessed a certain magic, the magic of being lost in being lost. Historically, this particular magic had kept me guessing the hidden structure of someone else's design.

Now I refused this magic; it wasn't my circus, as Jess said, to figure out what Chuck felt.

40. What exactly is an empty house?

I spent much of the next forty-eight hours at the hospital, anticipating the questions I'd have to answer at grand rounds. What was your anesthetic plan? At the first signs of bradycardia, how did you manage the competing half-lives?

And then, finally, it was Saturday morning, and they were late for their flight.

"Do you even know what happens at a funeral?" I asked Jess.

She eye-rolled me. Something had twisted her through this week—not just the miscarriage, but something at the corn maze.

The rattlesnake terrier started digging up some dirt by the base of the treehouse. Dr. Watermelon told Jess to draw in her elbows and he carried her to his car.

"I don't understand," Chuck whispered. "We've never slept apart like this. It feels shameful."

"I hope you'll talk to me when you come back," I said.

After they drove off, I relearned that an empty house was a compilation of hinged stretches of varying airlessness. An organ slice of physical and emotional resonances that we claw desperately at, to collect the fading purple-red glow of their heat.

I felt devastated and free. This aloneness, just me and the nest of ants that lived below our pantry. Perhaps in my old age, I'd learn to communicate with bees, wear that great white mask, invite the swarm to gather around my face.

I wanted to do something that I wanted to do. Uninvited, I drove over to Lacey's for a mimosa, which her six-year-old son would prepare for us, proud of the sprig of mint he'd set on the rim of the glass. Lacey, I figured, would instruct me to take a week or two on Orcas, where she had a few old kayaks, covered in cobwebs. If my stitches held, I could drag one down to the shore, glide past the orange and purple starfish suckered to their rocks.

41. Why did you become an anesthesiologist?

On a whim, I stopped at some city park. Open space, a softball diamond, a fountain in the middle of an algae pond. Pleasant. I walked through groups of African Americans preparing their cookouts. Someone was wearing a purple corduroy hat that said *Gengar 094*, whatever that meant. I heard the reassuring hum of power lines, which reminded me of me, endlessly circling the electrical towers, contriving a scheme to provoke my grandma into speech.

Chloroform, I read at the public library, put people in a drunken, twilight state upon waking.

After Grandma woke, I would ask about my parents, and Grandma would tell me the truth.

I convinced the Girl Moriarties to help me break into the chemistry lab at school. At the dollar store, I bought a set of dish towels with different kinds of mushrooms on them.

Grandpa had gone out to bowl; Grandma was watching *Guiding Light*. I snuck up behind her, pressed the chloroform-soaked towel to her nose and mouth.

She went limp almost immediately. She snored. I heard her slow breath. I waited.

"Such a dreamless nap," she said. This was about an hour later. "My throat is parched."

I got her some lemonade. I put it in her favorite glass, a tourist souvenir from Reno, Nevada, dotted with brightly colored hot air balloons.

"Where's Mom and Dad?" I said sweetly.

"Dear child, I don't know. I wish I did."

"Like Wonder Woman's lasso, you are compelled to tell me."

"Gracey, I honestly have no idea. On my heart, I would have told you a long time ago."

The maze I drew that night had no entrance or exit. I was irretrievable to myself. Then, a week later, my parents came home. They looked the same. They ruffled my hair. They took me to the waterslide.

So, I figured, the chloroform did signal them back.

So, you ask, why anesthesiology?

Because the magic of sleep is a bargain, a beacon, an alchemy, a concoction.

Because anesthesiology has always been about control of the body, controlling the removal of the body from the self, and when, and why.

42. Why did you invite Moreland to the house?

I realized that the cartographer's death had tripped a circuit I couldn't flip back by myself.

"Drink," he said that evening. He had joined some whiskey-of-the-month club that delivered a red, unmarked box to his porch; the bottle of single malt had been packed in the shredded paper of greyhound races. It excited him; it felt illicit.

Upstairs, Russell had closed the door to his bedroom. I could hear his stereo, playing the Fiery Lips or the On Fire Lips, crooning about robots and vitamins, about heroes saving the febrile world.

While I pulled out the whiskey tumblers, I watched Moreland assessing the house. Chuck's collection of signed baseballs, the daffodils on each throw pillow? Nothing here was special—undoubtedly we had a shorter driveway, flocks of more banal birds winging overhead.

He didn't seem to mind. He talked about his daughter, and how even Roger Federer couldn't stop getting older, not even with hyperbaric chambers and bone broth.

It felt good to listen to him ramble about quotidian things. Still, I couldn't help bringing up the case.

"Grace," he said.

"Why can't I solve it?"

"Do you want to take the lead for grand rounds? Will that make you feel more in control?"

"I can't help but feeling like we could have saved him."

"Not with our knowledge, we couldn't."

"Then what could we have done?"

"We are public servants!" he said. It startled me, that he thought of himself that way, and that he was chastising me. "We can't let ourselves be paralyzed by our humiliations!"

"Okay," I said. "Let's talk like humans again, not like doctors."

43. You told Moreland about Angels Landing?

He poured me a double, and I remembered how Jess, probably asleep by now in the hotel room, wanted to 3-D print ice-cube trays with the outline of giant flies.

At some point, Moreland mentioned that his wife was phobic about heights.

"Me and Chuck went to Utah once," I said. "Before we had kids, we fancied ourselves actual campers, meaning that we had rented a propane stove for our dehydrated chili."

"Some might call that hardcore."

"We certainly did. You ever heard of this hike called Angels Landing? Scariest, shittiest, most exhilarating thing I've ever done. On one side, there's a vertical drop, thousands of feet, I'm talking certain death, and you have to hang on to chain links nailed into the face of the rock. Halfway through, I froze. I looked up, because I couldn't bear to look down. I saw the thinnest, bluest sky above, and a single hawk spiraling. My brain was completely incapable of sending signals to my muscles. I remember even having the impulse to let go of the chain."

"Once I had that thought on a ski lift," Moreland said. "Just jump off. It made no sense."

"There has to be some self-destructive impulse at the pit of us. Anyway, Chuck must have noticed, because he squeezed my shoulder, roughly, like the first compression of a blood pressure cuff. 'Okay, Grace,' I said to myself. 'Get on the horse.' I took a moment to scratch at the mountain. For some reason I wanted its particles under my nails, a souvenir or something, and then I moved up the chain."

"Was the view worth it? After you almost got yourself killed?"

"We shared the summit with a bunch of aggressively hungry chipmunks," I said. "But what I remember most is how time had stopped. I heard every single echo of that hawk's voracious call, even the sound of air rippling above its wings. We don't get to experience that very often, do we? Almost never, and I knew it. That was the night I first talked to Chuck about having children. I would make sure that they would be open to what I felt at Angels

Landing, to the transcendent bits the world had to offer. And I think I did good with my kids, more or less. But then why was Beatrice ripped away? What did I do wrong? Was it the moments of my ambivalence or selfishness? Was the miscarriage the baby's way of saying she didn't want to be here with me?"

44. How did Moreland respond?

He didn't mind me wiping my snot on the pillow.

"You are not a cold, collapsed star," he said.

45. What brought you back to normal time?

After a while, I heard the rattlesnake terrier gnawing comically at his forepaw.

"Sorry," I said. "I must be the rambling kind of drunk."

"It's okay. Though I should take off—I told Marion I'd be home a few hours ago."

At the front door, he hugged me. It was the nicest physical contact I had had in a long time. I felt all five of his fingers on my back. I felt my chest against his. It scared me, as if I wasn't allowed to feel this pleasure from a man who wasn't my husband.

Eventually he pressed a button on his keys; his car turned on. "We're doing a double hip on Tuesday," he said. "I checked the schedule."

"See you then," I said. I waved goodbye.

46. You felt better after he left?

I gathered my case notes off the coffee table and I reread them and I felt the whiskey run hot down the esophagus and I didn't feel like I'd have to read them again.

47. There was something out front?

Yeah, my son sneaking up the ladder to the treehouse. From there, he walked along a thick branch, clambered through his bedroom window, into his room. Evidently he had broken his restriction. Like the tooth fairy, I thought, when he slept, I'd set a note under his pillow to express how deeply abandoned I felt.

Ever since the miscarriage, the contrails of everyone's grief everywhere, gridding up my sky.

Except I didn't feel abandoned. I felt relief. At least Russell had the wherewithal to deal with his feelings out of earshot.

What was it about the treehouse that, after years of disuse, attracted both my children? We had built it to placate Jess after the rabid dog. Did it comfort her, the way she could spy on everything from between the planks?

It was strangely warm outside. As I started to climb, I could feel my stitches tugging slightly; my fingers took the splinters in the rungs. A few empty cans of root beer on the treehouse floor, and a transistor radio I think I had once won.

I could smell the oak.

I looked down. I saw the tangle of the uncoiled garden hose, the glow of the doorbell. For a moment, our house looked like a house again.

48. Why did you feel the need to conduct this interview?

So I could live outside and inside and outside myself, act as one's own ghost and ghostwriter, pass through myself as a hand punches through mist.

ROBERT GLICK *is Associate Professor of English at the Rochester Institute of Technology, where he teaches creative writing and electronic literature. "Questions for Anesthesiologists" is an excerpt from his current project, the novel* The Paradox of Wonder Woman's Airplane. *Standalone sections from this novel have won the Summer Literary Seminars and the* New Ohio Review *fiction competitions, and others have been published in* The Collagist *and the* Los Angeles Review. *His first collection of stories is forthcoming from C&R Press in 2019.*

Doctor, Doctor, Doctor

Blair Lee

The doctor finds some abnormal endometrial cells on my cervix when I do my woman's wellness exam and sends a biopsy off to a lab somewhere in Western North Carolina. It's for my employer's health-and-wellness plan. We're all automatically entered into a drawing and the winner gets a five-thousand-dollar travel voucher to anywhere in the world, so long as they go through Triple A travel agency. I could have avoided the doctor all together, even though Marc's been asking me to go. Not made a New Year's resolution like my friends do. Erin, for instance, promises herself to lose forty pounds in four months. Hayley's cutting sweets; Sabrina, gluten. Neither is for the weight loss, they say, but for their health. Even the barrel-stomached lumberjack of an HR rep, Steve, is going to the gym twice a week. *For my health*, he says, and if he happens to lose some weight while at it, all the better.

The doctor asks if I have any pain and I tell her not really, maybe a bit during sex. And if I lie on my back. Sometimes my side, too, but mostly just during sex and a bit afterward. Sometimes I throw up and bleed after sex, sometimes during.

I don't particularly *like* sex, I tell the doctor.

She sits behind her laptop on an adjustable swivel barstool and raises an eyebrow. She types. *Uh, huh,* she says, and enters something in her computer with a slow nod. I can imagine her typing—

COMMENTS: *Hates sex so much she throws up. Strange woman. Left nipple slightly more glandular than right. No breast lumps, but doesn't like sex. Doesn't like sex? Doesn't like sex. Enter code G89.29: Other chronic pain. Mostly other. Very strange.*

She asks again if I've only ever been with my current partner. My husband, I say, yes. Only him. And he only with me. We married young. Twenty. Been together ten years.

Right, she says, typing. Do you mind if we do another manual exam?

I say *sure* and lean back. My pants and underwear are already off under a thin white sheet like I'm an old piece of furniture and I make a little tent when I prop my legs up in the stirrups.

Some cold lubricant, the doctor says, and she inserts two fingers into my vagina. She presses down on my lower stomach and works her fingers into the deep left of my cavity.

Any pain?

No.

She presses on. Any pain? Pain? All the way over to my right side and my ass cheeks clench and I jump a little on the table.

Painful?

A bit, I say.

She snaps off her gloves and presses my knees down flat. I knew I was coming today. I should have shaved. I should have wiped down with a wet paper towel or a baby wipe or something, anything, and caught the toilet paper that collects along either canal of my labium like a lint trap. The doctor's an attractive woman and young for a doctor. I can't help but wonder what she thinks of me.

I'm going to send you a referral to Allison, she says, over at Raleigh Triangle Physical Therapy. She works specifically with women's issues. Really great. With the angle of your pain, I'm wondering if it might be muscle-related . . . Are your periods regular?

I don't know, I say, and sit up on the white crinkle paper. The lubricant is warm now and seeps out my vagina. Probably every few months.

Months?

They haven't always been that way, I say. They used to be non-stop. Bleeding all the time.

She tosses the vaginal gloves into *hazardous waste*.

Do you only get pain with sex? she asks.

No, I admit.

Like when you go to the bathroom? she asks.

When I poop? Sometimes. I can't really tell.

She types again into her computer. I'm going to schedule you for an ultrasound, she says. See if we can't figure out what's going on in there.

She glances to my vagina when she says *in there*. I do, too. Like somehow my vagina made an active decision to fuck up.

* * *

I take a half day on Friday for the doctor's.

Where you goin'? Erin asks. She eats carrots with watered down hummus. She says she's lost five pounds this week.

I lick the sugar from the bottom of a vending machine pack of Sour Patch Kids and then suck each finger before throwing the wrapping away. I squeeze some antibacterial onto my hands and rub them together like a chipmunk.

Women problems, I say, and she tosses her head back and rolls her eyes. Erin's worked as a medical coder at this campus of WakeMed for eight years and still has far more enthusiasm for it than I do, even though I've only been here for three.

Mmmph, she says, I'm sorry.

It'll be fine. I shake my head. But vaginas, am I right?

Right? she says. Because, really, we both know I'm not entirely joking.

* * *

I like the ultrasound more than I care to admit. The room is dark and I feel like I'm in the bowels of a boat somewhere far off at sea. I pretend the Battleship–style monitor is our navigation and when the ultrasound tech turns on the volume to hear the blood flow to my ovaries, I like to think she's a sonar technician. Mostly, though, with the warm jelly and the slow rolling of the ultrasound wand atop my stomach, I pretend that I'm pregnant. I don't ever admit to anyone that I want kids because when I first got married, I didn't.

Then the ultrasound tech asks me to empty my bladder. I do, in the florescent adjoining bathroom, and when I get back into the dark of our room I'm immediately comforted.

We're going to do the internal now, she says, and squeezes some warm lubricant atop the probe. She's got a soft southern accent and the room is dark and I say okay and let my legs fall open. Then the probe goes in and she presses sharp right with the wand and things get real serious.

*   *   *

Endometriosis. Polycystic Ovarian Syndrome. Prediabetes. At least it's not cancer. The doctor was worried about that, with the bleeding. I take an entire week to plan out when I want to tell Marc. Take him on a walk, Erin suggests. She's down ten pounds now in just a week and throws away my Sour Patch Kids when I'm not looking. I tell her he doesn't like the outdoors, but maybe I'll take him to sushi or something, that's his favorite. She says I'll have to watch my carbs, now, with the prediabetes and all. Erin's got a stack of wellness books on her desk tall as her lamp, but I don't think she's actually read any of them despite her constant outpouring of unsolicited health advice.

When I get home I dress up for sushi and take a piece of printer paper and quarter a makeshift Valentine's card. I wonder if, some-where deep inside, I planned for these two events to coincide. We never celebrate Valentine's Day, but I think maybe now will be a nice time to start. Marcus disagrees. I can tell he's annoyed I made a card at all, but he at least agrees to go to sushi on account of it being good, not on the account of it being Valentine's Day. I say that's good, it'll be nice to talk, and the way he glances at me from the corners of his eyes lets me know he already suspects something.

*   *   *

I should have known, too, that the restaurant would be crowded given the day of the month. We get the last table available, a square one in an aisleway. There's no corner or wall for either of us to back into, but neither of us wanted to wait forty minutes, either. The expanse makes me feel like I'm sitting with a stranger, all dressed up with something on my mind. We order edamame and tea and we look over the sushi menu, which is not half off today. I keep waiting for a time to open up the conversation, but Marc's too into the menu and the restaurant is abnormally loud and then the waiter comes back with our water, then tea, then sushi plates, then edamame. Marc's finally ready to order, and we order three rolls each: dynamite, caterpillar, wolf; green dragon, yasai, avocado. Then it's just us and the edamame and I suck the salt off a pod, squeeze the slick beans out with my tongue. Marcus checks his phone. I stare at a young couple in a lucky booth seat. They hold hands across the table and lean into each other's conversation.

Marcus and I are used to silence. We get along when we talk, but we also get along fine when we don't. When we finish the edamame down to a pile of empty sacks, I lick the tips of my fingers and dry them with the cloth napkin. Marcus and I stare at each other and smile contently. Then I say:

I think I want a kid.

He laughs. I must be joking. Surely, I must be joking. Wait, he says, Allie. Are you serious? Because if you are, this is something we need to talk about.

I know I want a kid, I say again. Maybe two. Girls, actually. If I can help it.

Where is this coming from? he asks.

I've wanted it for a while, I say. I just didn't want to mess anything up. Mess us up.

You seriously want kids?

I have endometriosis, Marc. Polycystic ovarian syndrome. Prediabetes. I'm thirty. It'll take longer for me to get pregnant, and time is already—

Wait, wait, he says. What? I can't hear you.

I repeat again, louder. I'm basically screaming.

What do you have? he asks. When did all this happen?

Poor, poor Marc. I don't say this, but I look at him in a way that oozes pity. Poor Marc. Poor husband. Poor man. His eyes are so open now, staring at me. Waiting.

Endometriosis, I say. Polycystic ovarian syndrome. Prediabetes.

I get the prediabetes.

Yeah.

What else?

Endometriosis. Polycystic ovarian syndrome.

I like how endometriosis sounds out loud. And polycystic. Almost enjoyable until you get to the mundanity of ovarian and syndrome.

It sounds more exotic than it is, I tell him. Really, I'll be fine. But it'll be harder for me.

To have kids, he clarifies.

Right, I say, then explain to him what endometriosis and PCOS is. He only seems to half-follow along. There's a kind of vacancy in his face. A flatness, like a painting, like he's already a third gone.

Babe, he says. I'm sorry. I just don't want kids. Still, he says. Ever.

My eyes burn.

I know, I say.

I'm sorry, he says again. I nod. I know.

I love you, he says.

I love you, too, I say.

Our waiter comes back with our boat of sushi. It's literally a wooden boat. We got a big ol' love boat here, he says, and sets it down in the center of our table. At some point, he must have taken our slobbery edamame pods, because they've disappeared. And then he smiles at Marcus, says, Enjoy, smiles at me too. I'm actually crying now and the waiter leaves before I blow my nose into the fancy cloth napkin.

* * *

Erin is the first person I tell about the divorce, but after I tell her to stop throwing away my Sour Patch Kids. You know how much money you've thrown away? I ask. A lot, I tell her, in case she doesn't know. Like, a lot.

Allie, it's better for you, she says. Most these food dyes are illegal in other first-world countries.

She's down fifteen pounds, now.

All of this will be better for you, she says. It'll just take time. Everything takes time. Aren't you glad though? she asks. That you went to the doctor?

Not really, I say. Maybe not at all, actually.

We walk around the hospital. Last summer, they put in a new sidewalk that circles the whole facility. This spring they've planted new trees. Red and pink and white crape myrtles. They still have the little plastic tubes on for support, the wire anchors for when it gets windy. For when the maintenance guys accidentally run into them.

You look like you've lost weight, she says. Have you been trying?

No, I say. But yeah, I've noticed a difference.

Lucky, she says. You look good. I mean, you were fine before, but you look good.

Erin adjusts the band of her pants to fit just on top of her lower stomach roll and waddles her pant legs back into place like she's a duck out of water.

How's Marcus? she asks.

He's okay, I say. Bad, I add. Really depressed, actually. But he'll be okay. I've never seen him cry so much. I feel kind of awful. But I think this will be better for him, too, in the long run.

It's all about the long run, Erin agrees.

He's gonna go back for his master's degree.

Oh wow, she says. That's nice.

We walk a while in silence. I haven't eaten breakfast and decided to skip lunch to walk with Erin. My stomach caves itself inward, but I ignore it, push on, take a drink from my water. We pass the main doors to the hospital again and a woman walks out. She holds the hand of a little girl, who steps in dramatic arches so that her shoes light up with each stomp. Come on, Jaena, the woman says, two steps ahead of the little girl, her arm trailed behind her like string to a kite.

I've got a spin class tonight, Erin says, in Durham, if you want to come with me. It's kind of therapeutic. Might even be good to just get you out of the house.

Yeah, I say. Might be nice. Yeah . . . I mean, we still love each other—which actually makes it harder.

Sure, Erin says, sure. Like she doesn't believe me.

*   *   *

The physical therapist gives me another manual exam. With her fingers deep in my vagina, she asks me when it hurts.

I tell her what I told my last doctor.

Hmm. Does it hurt when your husband touches your clitoris? she asks.

Um, I laugh a little beneath my breath. She readjusts the angles of her fingers. I wouldn't know, I finally say.

You wouldn't know? she asks.

No, I say.

She takes out her fingers and rolls a little away. She makes a face of astonishment and tosses her gloves out.

You need to teach him some things, she says. Really—she laughs, now, too—that's not okay.

Poor Marcus.

Really, I say, it doesn't matter anyways. We're separating. Getting divorced.

She tells me to turn to my side. Well, I mean, I almost hate to say it, but that might be better for you, she says. Then she sticks one probe on my right ass cheek and two on either side of my anus.

We're going to measure your pelvic floor, she says.

My legs, again, are under a white sheet.

Give your cheeks a squeeze, she says, make sure the electrodes are on there nice and good.

I squeeze my cheeks and watch her computer. It records my pelvic muscles like a seismograph. My peaks are at the top of the chart.

Relax, she says.

I try.

She turns off the lights and puts a pillow beneath my knees. Better? she asks.

I can't tell a difference, so I nod.

Relax, she says again.

I try. She asks me to turn on my side so my bare ass points toward her. She checks the electrodes and asks me to lay on my back again—asks me to relax again. You're really tense, she says. Have you ever experienced any abuse? she asks. Physical or emotional?

I shake my head *no*.

Do you *enjoy* sex?

I mean, it's *okay*, I say, with an emphasis on the okay that suggests maybe it isn't.

Hmm, she says. I might have you go see Doctor Nancy at Wake County Counseling. This could be something psychological. Everything is so connected, she says, and motions toward her body as an example. The mind and body. If something up here—she taps her head—isn't letting go, it can affect something else in here—she motions again at the rest of her body. But you definitely have some tension, she says, and circles her hand in the air above my pelvis like she's directing energy through my chakra.

She opens up another screen on her computer that starts counting down. Let's see if we can't fatigue those pelvic muscles, she says.

* * *

Marcus and I go through the garage. It's still cold and damp, early March, and I hug my sweater close to my body.

Maybe if we'd bought a house, I say, we would have stayed together.

What do you mean? he asks.

Instead of renting, I say.

I know that. But why?

Because, I shrug. We'd be kind of stuck together.

People with houses get divorced all the time.

He moves the lawnmower backward in a way that makes his triceps bulge. A line cuts through the muscles of his forearm. Marc's got a well-formed back. Broad shoulders and a narrow waist. It would have been a good trait to pass down. I take my time looking, trying to hold onto as much as possible. No ass, though.

You want to sell the table saw? he asks, and pulls the cover off the giant table saw in the corner of our garage.

You don't want it?

I've got a studio. What am I gonna do with a table saw?

You can keep it here, if you want.

I bought him that table saw five Christmases ago and I don't like the idea of someone else having it, even though it only ever got used once. He wipes off some dust and puts the cover back on.

I feel like that's not healthy, he says.

Why? I ask. We're still friends. I've got the space.

It's going to be hard enough for me, he says, without having half of my stuff with you.

I frown. It's involuntary, mostly. I haven't cried in four days, which is my longest record so far, and I don't want to ruin it.

I'm going to miss you, I say, and grab onto his eyes with mine.

I'm going to miss you, too.

*   *   *

Don't stop.

I'm crying again. Marc's taken the bedframe to the studio and he's naked atop me and the mattress on our bedroom floor. It's a symbol of our transition. The lights are off. The blinds are closed, but light still seeps through the slats. The lines cut Marc's body into contrasting horizontal strips.

But you're crying, he says.

I know. Keep going.

He looks at my face and then closes his eyes, thrusts his body over and over into mine. He's uncertain at first, but eventually, he gains momentum.

This is our last time.

I close my eyes, too, squeeze the tears from my eyes and grab onto his shoulder. I press my lips into the triangle between his collarbone and neck and rock my hips against his.

It hurts more than usual and I can feel the bones of my pelvis grate against his. I shouldn't have lost so much weight. Even if for this moment. Or maybe, I deserve all of this pain—the hurt in my head and heart and bones and soul.

I accidentally let slip a cry. Sniff in.

No, don't stop.

I want to be one with him, one last time, even if it doesn't feel good. I breathe in his shoulder and wish it wouldn't hurt so much.

He gasps and pulls himself out. I open my eyes. It's over already and we both watch in anticipation as the liquid pearl pools onto my stomach, marbled with a thin swirl of blood.

*   *   *

I've been crying less since I've stopped eating solid food. Erin's on a liquid detox and down thirty pounds and I've noticed I'm more emotionally stable now since the initial mood swings. I stick mostly to vegetable-based smoothies so it doesn't spike my glucose, and for the most part I feel as emotionally stable as a blank sheet of paper. It makes me feel good, not needing food. Being above it.

Marc's voiced concern multiple times.

The counselor, sitting across from me in a room with furniture and native-patterned blankets and a miniature rock garden on the windowsill (probably purchased from Amazon or Walmart), asks if I feel as though I'm experiencing a loss. Which, of course, I am. Then she asks if I've noticed any physical reaction to this loss.

I cry, I say.

Okay, she says, and nods and waits. This isn't good enough, I can tell, for her. Anything else?

My physical therapist says I'm holding onto stress in my vagina.

I don't tell her the details. About what, exactly happens—or doesn't—with Marc. That Dr. Brie had wanted me to fatigue my own muscles—strengthen my pelvic floor. Climax on my own.

That I could hardly even think about touching myself, let alone do anything about it.

Is she the one who recommended you come here?

I nod. My OBGYN suggested I go to the physical therapist. The physical therapist suggested I come here.

Well the mind and body are extremely interconnected, she says, and moves her hand in an elliptical *wax-on* motion in front of her torso. So it's very possible. Do you notice any other responses in your body?

I shrug. Not really.

How's your diet and exercise?

I've got prediabetes, I say. So I've been watching out for that. And my best friend at work is trying to lose weight, so I'm helping with that, too.

Helping her lose weight?

Yeah, kind of. I mean I'm just going with her when she does things. Walking and cycling and all that.

How do you feel about your body?

I stare at her grey eyes without blinking. In the past ten years, I haven't given this much thought.

Fine? I ask.

So you feel good where your body is right now? Weight gain or loss or shape or size?

Mostly, yeah.

How often do you exercise? she asks.

My insides bristle. I don't know. Whenever my friend wants to. I don't really think about it.

How often would you say that is? she asks.

Once a day during the weekday, I say. Sometimes twice.

Sometimes twice, she says, and I don't like how she repeats it. A burst of sweat pushes out my pores.

I've noticed a change in your posture, she says. How are you feeling right now?

I don't know, I tell her. Fine. I don't tell her: Good. In control. Better than . . . something. Better than everyone else? Better than myself?

*   *   *

I am a god. I sit in a line of traffic calm as ice. All day, I've only had water. On top of it, I'm almost an hour early for SoulCycling with Erin. Mostly, though, I just feel a bit numb. I'm never early and I think I can get used to this feeling. One third of my house is gone and I consider stopping at Target to look around.

The light goes green. I stare at the red circles, one inside the other, and swing a right. Someone behind me beeps, but I make the turn, think: you cannot get to me here. You cannot get to me inside my body, inside my mind.

*   *   *

At some point it's turned to Easter season. I don't know, at all, when Easter is. Maybe I've been too busy, or too tired, or too filled with my new way of living. But Target is filled with Easter. Mostly, Easter candy. It's all set out row by row as soon as you enter the store. You can smell the sugar through the factory-sealed plastic. Of course I have to stop. I love Target with all the red and white and gray. How their carts and baskets have a thicker, rounder plastic. I love that they always have the best selection of candy, especially during the holidays. I love the way the candy smells, the way the packaging crinkles when you pick it up. It's the experience of Christmas each time, except with no parents to tell you *no*, to say, *put that back*, or *that's enough*.

I immediately start filling my basket. It's a habit and everything is so brightly colored and the daylight still makes its way in from the storefront of doors. A woman browses next to me, and I try to ignore her. She's got her hair up in a ponytail and wears yoga pants with a tightly fitted zip-up. You can tell that she's a mom, the way she looks over the aisle like she owns it, with such determinism and such *I-don't-give-a-fuck*-ness. This is a woman who has to deal with the constant stress of other mothers on a regular basis. One that organizes field trips and bake sales and maybe works part- or full-time and also—considering her ring—has to take care of a husband at home. She's got it all, and would be underappreciated if she didn't complain about being underappreciated all the time. I bet she lost her baby weight a month after birth. Like the celebrity tabloids advertise.

She makes me self-conscious and it increases my indecision. Chocolate or fruit tootsie rolls? Maybe both? Reese's has come out with yellow-dyed egg-shaped candy, now, too, and Twizzlers has green apple-flavored pull and peels that have already been pulled and peeled to resemble grass. The woman grabs a bag of Jolly Rancher jelly beans, bunny-and-chick Peeps in four total colors, the Reese's that are not shaped like two-dimensional eggs, but smaller three-dimensional eggs, and two chocolate shell bunnies wrapped in gold. One has a pink ribbon painted across the foil, the other, blue.

Then she gives a tight-lipped smile as she walks in front of me to leave the aisle. When she does, I look down at my clothes. At my now oversized perspiration-stained workout t-shirt and yoga pants. They used to make my ass look fantastic at one point in time. The other day, Marcus had mentioned how small my ass has become. Boobs, too, he added, but the problem is that I didn't care until now, seeing this woman. I put four packages of Peeps into my basket, and two shell bunnies, like I, too, have children, and then I add what I really want. The Reese's, the Twix, the tootsie rolls (both flavors), the Twizzler grass, and, lastly, a small bag of Robin's Eggs, which is the only consistency, the only thing to look the same as they do every year.

* * *

Nothing can reach me at SoulCycle. I pound the pedals with Alex, our brave leader, heading the front of the room. I know the routine by heart. The lights are down and my heart rate is up. I try to push aside thoughts of the candy sitting in my car.

Let's go! Alex shouts.

Whoo! I tilt my head back and return the cry.

My feet keep beating, beating, beating. My legs pump furiously, my pelvis teeters back and forth. I grab my sports bottle and squirt water into my mouth like a marathoner. It pours down my face, mixes with my sweat. I can feel the liquid snake down and land in the empty basket of my stomach. Erin glances over at me. The droplets slide down my neck. I think: I am from water. I am water. Water will purify me from inside and out.

*   *   *

Do you want the two-quart or four-quart?

Marcus holds the two pots in his hands, again emphasizing the creases in his forearms and the bulges of his biceps. I like his arms. And his hands. And his face.

Two? I ask. Four? Which do you want?

Babe, he says, I don't care. I don't cook.

I'll take the two, I say.

You'll probably have people over more than me.

I won't, I say.

You sure?

I nod and Marcus adds the four-quarter to his box labeled *kitchen*. We've already divided the bathroom and this is his final box. My candy sits on the counter. I've taken it all out, spread it on the counter like a kind of alter. When I walk by, I make sure to look at each package, feel the plush of the Peeps with my fingers, imagine sinking my teeth into a raspberry tootsie roll. Then I fill a glass of water and walk by, think: You're doing so well. You're doing so well.

I ask if he wants the Keurig.

I got that for you, he says. And I don't even drink coffee.

That's right, I say, and open the drawer of silver wear. Should we just halve this?

He slips the four-quarter lid into the side of the box. The handle pushes a wave into the cardboard and he shrugs.

So I begin the process. One spoon for him, one for me, one fork for him, one for me, one knife for him, one for me, like pulling apart Noah's ark.

We negotiate with the ladles and spatulas and whisks. I keep the pie cutter. He gets the cheese grater. He takes the toaster but I get the blender. There are so many sharp things in a kitchen. We both pause when I hold up the can opener.

Marcus doesn't shrug. Neither do I.

It's a good can opener, I say.

It is, he agrees. He still kneels by his final box.

It's the first thing we got together, at a Rite Aid in San Diego, when we lived in a hotel for a month while trying to find housing. Ten years, and it still works like the very first day.

Hardly any rust, I acknowledge, like how someone might make an observation about a deceased coworker at a funeral.

And it opens bottles, Marcus points out.

It does. Doesn't do that skippy bullshit either.

Mmm.

You can have it, I say, and think: Add it to my list of sacrifices.

Babe, he says, and stands up. He takes my hands in his and closes my fingers around the can opener, around its smooth black handles. Really, he says, you can have it if you want.

No, no, I say. You're starting new. This is one less thing you have to worry about. It's reliable. It'll make me feel better, if you have it.

You'll probably use it more.

No, I say, I won't. Really, Marc. Please. Take it.

I gently push our group of hands into his chest. I keep it there, our hands enclosed like we're protecting something sacred, like keeping safe a baby bird, maybe, or the combination of our hearts.

I can just get a new one. It's no big deal, I say. Though, clearly it's a big deal for both of us.

He blinks, some spell of mine broken. His shoulders drop.

I want a new one, he says, like he's just realized this.

No, I say, you want *this* one.

No, he says again, I want a *new* one.

Well what about this one? I ask.

You can have this one, he says. Really, babe, it's no big deal.

He opens the cupboard next. My heart drops. When he starts rummaging through the mixing bowls I shove the rusted can opener deep into the corner of his box.

*　　*　　*

Erin's won the five-thousand-dollar giveaway at work. We think the nurses hate her, but even the schedulers and other coders seem too happy to be genuine. Only Steve seems to have a legitimate response. His wife's recently been diagnosed with breast cancer and he's ballooned up over the last two months.

I can't imagine having that money for a trip, he tells Erin between bites of a jelly-filled at lunch. Take Jemma somewhere real nice. Late honeymoon or something, you know? Like they say, better late than never.

Erin nods while doing a sort of indecisive shrug back and forth with her head. There's no good way to answer Steve, and she and I both know it. I watch for a response from her instead of interjecting, until it gets uncomfortable enough for me to ask Erin on a walk outside.

*   *   *

I feel bad for Steve, she says on our second lap around the hospital.

I do too, I say. Everyone does.

But I still want to keep the trip.

You won it, I say. You should keep it. It's probably not even transferable, I say, even though I have no idea if this is true.

It's a trip for two, she says. Which makes me feel even worse. Pat is sucking up real bad, though. I can tell. She's mentioned Ireland. Says she's always wanted to go.

You can't make everyone happy, I say. I notice, while we walk, that Erin's face looks a little puffier. Her hips, too, seem to stretch at her pants.

Would you want to go? she asks. Wherever? I haven't thought of where yet.

Oh, wow, I say. Are you sure?

She nods. Of course.

Then yeah, I say, sure. Thanks. That'd be awesome.

Good, she says, with a smile that makes it seem like we've bonded. Want to maybe get dinner tonight? Instead of cycling? Have a little celebration?

I hesitate.

We don't have to, she says. Just an idea.

I just feel like you've been doing really well lately, I say. And it's so hard to start up again when you've stopped. Plus, I already told Alex we'd be there.

Erin doesn't hide the disappointment in her face. She takes a sip from her mint-infused water. That's fine, she says. Allie?

Mm?

You doing all right? I mean . . . I haven't been wanting to say anything, but everyone's been talking.

About what? I ask.

You just look . . . worn. Thin, she says.

It's not like I've meant to, I say.

I know, it's just—it's dangerous. Losing that much weight. I mean, we work at a hospital—it's just. We think about your health. You know?

I *do* know.

Okay, she says. Her eyebrows raise. Her voice, too, shifts up an octave. I study her face, my irritation mirrored. The conversation, clearly, is over.

*   *   *

It's been twenty-four hours, now, at ten p.m. A full twenty-four hours alone in our house. My house, now. I couldn't sleep at all and marched for seven hours straight in place. It's been three days since I've had anything other than water. Since ten p.m. last night, I've walked through the kitchen over twenty times and then lost count. I stood in front of my shrine of candy each time, stared at all the bright colors, touched all the different packaging, ushered the surrounding sugar-air into my nose like fanning incense at an altar.

Marc hasn't called or texted. I want to not want him to.

I go to the bathroom and stand naked in front of the mirror. Hot bathwater fills the tub, equal parts loud and relaxing. I think of the woman at Target. I stare at the ant mounds of my breasts, the lopsided feathers of my ribs, admire how my hip bones jut out so far you could grab one and pull my body apart. From the side, my shoulder blades look like wings.

The water quiets, nearing the top of the tub, and I turn it off, slip my body into the waves of hot water. It burns all over. My ass bones dig into the hard iron of the tub and I lean my head back against the tile and close my eyes.

I stay like this for some time, let my arms go so they drift up partway to the surface. It's been a while since I've meditated. The PT doctor's been wanting me to do this more, relax so that my pelvic muscles relax, and after I've fully relaxed, work on my Kegels. I keep my eyes shut and pull water into my vagina. It rushes in like high tide and I expel it back out into the ocean of my tub. I clench my pelvic floor and let go, then pull water in again. I let the water sit in me and wonder if I can get it up through my cervical opening before pushing it out again. It's cleansing. Therapeutic. I let the water fill my insides again and then keep my pelvis relaxed, let the warmth flow naturally in and out as it pleases.

I open my eyes and—for a moment—look down at a body that does not feel like mine. My hands and arms are strangely disconnected, the uneven rippling of my skin through water moving a too-frail body in and out of focus. I think, maybe, if I don't feel like myself, I might be able to finally satisfy myself like how the doctor wants. Like, maybe, how I want. I adjust my tailbone so that it rests more comfortably against the iron and bow my head down so that my spine stops rubbing against the ceramic tile. When the water lulls to a gentle rocking, I snake my hand down between my legs and part my knees so they rest against either side of the tub. It's a strange feeling, touching myself, and at first I just rub slowly back and forth with the flat plane of my gathered fingers before parting my inner labia from my outer, splitting two fingers to either side, pressing a little harder, rubbing a little faster.

But it doesn't do anything.

I try adding a circular motion, massaging in an elliptical pattern before pressing the small fold away from my clitoris. I work at it with my mount of Saturn while my middle and ring fingers rake smooth and strong, deep between the gorges of my minora and majora. It starts as something almost beautiful in its attempted satisfaction before it quickly becomes desperate. Ugly, even. My arm slaps hideously at the water. The water, previously smooth, turns choppy. It creates its own noise, aided in my movement, like a slosh of water down a garbage disposal. I hear my doctor's voice: *an orgasm a day keeps the doctor away.* I wonder if my doctors could do this better. Any of them. My legs tense. My forehead wrinkles. I sit up a little, start crying, fucking myself with my own fingers to no result.

I stop.

My whole body is tired. It feels nothing. For a moment, I lean my head back against tile and let the saltwater flow up the ridge of my cheekbone and then down to my chin before it collects itself into a mass heavy enough to drip back in with the rest of the water.

*   *   *

I walk to the kitchen dripping and naked like the female protagonist in some awful French film.

I think: Enter code G89.29. Other pain. Cannot even satisfy herself. The candy still sits untouched on the counter. My phone, beside it, is empty. No missed calls. No texts. No one waiting for me, wanting me back, wanting to know if I'm okay.

I breathe in the sugar air. Thoughtfully. Slowly.

Overtop the stiff plastic, my right fingers close around the head of a pink Peep. My left hand rubs the soft flat of my belly. I think, maybe, just one is okay. Correction. I think: Red Dye 40, aka Allura Red, a "reasonably anticipated" human carcinogen. Illegal, in most other first world countries. But most likely Red Dye 30, linked to thyroid cancer. ADHD. Changes in DNA. Illegal topically, but not orally.

I think, too, glucose and gelatin. Bone powder.

I split the serrated edge of plastic and tilt the white cardboard box that holds the little chicks like a boat. All the shimmering sugar pools into a corner, and I'm overcome with a desire to pour it over my body. Instead, I bring my head close to the cardboard, cradling it to my lips like a chalice of wine at communion. I stick my tongue into the corner and pull up a clump of sugar. My mouth floods with endorphins. The sugar dissolves and pulls back into the receding saliva of my throat.

I tear open the next package. Purple bunnies.

Red No. 3, Blue No. 1, Yellow No. 6. Potassium sorbate. More bone.

Already, my body expands. I suck the bunnies' heads off with the vacuum of my mouth, move onto the prepeeled Twizzlers. Glucose, glucose, wax, dye. I gag on one like a long noddle while I split open the bag of yellow Reese's.

Sugar. Dextrose. Emulsifier. TBHQ.

I've hardly unwrapped the second Reese's when I settle on the Robin Eggs. The packaging pulls me back in time. The happy colors, happy bird. I chew slower, read the back of the package: fractionated partially hydrogenated palm kernel oil, sodium bicarbonate, sorbitan tristearate soya lecithin, Yellow No. 5, Blue No. 1, Yellow No. 6, Red 40. My stomach hurts. My eyes burn. I pull apart the seal and reach into the bunch of eggs. Gently, I pluck one out. My mouth works to flush out the remaining Reese's and I rub the smooth of a white egg along my lips before sliding it in whole and washing over it with my tongue. The pockets of my cheeks ache. I suck on it a little while longer before moving the egg to the side of my molars and biting down. The hard shell breaks, the acid and enzymes in my saliva wash into the carcass and liquefy the malt. Soon, the whole egg crushes between the roof of my mouth and the weight of my tongue.

It's gone.

I reach back in, eat another. And another. And another. Then I'm grabbing them by the bunches, popping handfuls of eggs into my mouth, still wet and naked and hungrier than before. I think about Marc. I think about me, crushing eggshells between my teeth. I think about the potential of a potential child and shock shoots up my spine and through my tongue. I hope I won't feel this same way, that I can fill this hole. The malt dissolves down my throat. My stomach aches and my heart aches, and no matter how much I eat: the Peeps, Reese's, Twizzlers, eggs—all of it—I will always try desperately to feel full.

BLAIR LEE received her MFA in fiction from North Carolina State University and her MA in Literature from the University of Toledo. Her fiction and nonfiction have appeared in American Short Fiction, The Great Lakes Book Project, Bath Flash Fiction Volume 2, *and* The Penny Engine. *Her work has also been a finalist for the Cincinnati Review Robert and Adele Schiff Prize in Fiction, Glimmer Train's Fiction Contests, Omnidawn's Fabulist Fiction Chapbook Contest, and the VanderMey Nonfiction Prize. Currently, Blair is completing a collection of short stories focused on women's health and relationships, titled* Portrait of Another Woman.

Little Room

Carrie Grinstead

In the dream, Jessie ran to the barn to rescue horses from the flames. Her mom screamed. Nothing Grandma could do but sit by the kitchen window as the roof of the riding arena collapsed, and sparks tumbled to the starry sky.

It's finally happening, Jessie thought. This time it's real. It has to be real.

She awoke in silence at three thirty. No time to fall back to sleep before her alarm sentenced her to another day.

Down in the kitchen, chilly wind whistled low through the walls. Jessie pulled boots over pajama bottoms and rolled into her coat. Her mom, drinking coffee at the table, said, "Hot chocolate, Jess. I've been up half an hour already and I made your thermos of hot chocolate. Right there."

"I'm aware, Mother. I'm aware of the hot chocolate and if I want the hot chocolate I'll drink it."

"Well, don't you complain about the cold when I've got this all made and ready for you."

Jessie went outside, slamming the screen door. A lonely *woof* rose from Grandma's dog kennel. Full night still, and scattered stars turned the gravel silver. She flipped on the barn lights, horses snuffled in their stalls, and Jessie said, "Morning, assholes."

She carried two flakes of hay past Grimmie's stall. Grimmie, the ancient pony, was allergic to hay, and Jessie enjoyed taunting him with what he could not have. Grimmie would burn up in the fire and wouldn't care that he was burning up. Jessie tossed the hay to Milo, the sixteen-hand Dutch Warmblood who was privately owned by Elissa Pedersen, Jessie's classmate at the high school. Milo would survive. He had to because he was valuable. Easy Beat would make it out too. A sorrel quarter horse, bright as a new penny, he was the biggest asshole of them all, and they wouldn't even have to rescue him. It would be impossible for him to reach his great head over the stall door and use his teeth to undo the latch that kept him prisoner. Even so, Jessie believed he could do it and in fact believed he did. She suspected he got out every night, wandered around the property, and locked himself back in before morning.

She loaded a bin of grain onto a wheelbarrow and pushed it from stall to stall. A daddy long-legs, shimmering in the bare-bulb light, strolled past. Jessie's stomach heaved. Then, empty and cold as all the days before, angry as those to come, it swallowed her. She was echoing pain and hopeless desire. She was falling forever.

A cat appeared and placed a paw on four spider legs. The remaining legs danced for an instant, and then all vanished into the cat's mouth. The cat flinched and sneezed violently three times.

Jessie snickered. "Idiot. What did you think was going to happen."

*　*　*

Easy Beat once bucked Jessie off. He was two years old then, and she was still in junior high. He'd pranced and swished his tail and stuck his nose straight up in the air, and Mom had screamed, "Jesus Christ, Jessica, use your reins! Why are you letting him get away with that crap?"

There was still a crack in the arena wall where she'd hit it, butt first and upside down. Lying in the sawdust, spitting dirt, she'd watched Mom grab Easy's reins and back him up from one end of the arena to the other, punching his shoulders with a riding crop, rattling the bit in his teeth. He scooted back, back, back, ears flattened, eyes rolled wide. "Son of a bitch!" Mom hissed. "*Son of a bitch.*"

The week that followed was the greatest of Jessie's life. She stayed home from school, sitting on ice and watching TV. Grandma heated chicken soup for lunch and explained, "Mariah is the bad one. She says she came from Sweden, but that's all a lie. The accent is fake."

It was early fall then, still warm enough for open windows. Occasional deer wandered under orange trees. Grandma hit the side of the TV to make the picture sharper, even though they had cable now.

Jessie slept. God. She slept like she'd never slept before and might never sleep again. Twice she slept until noon, then slept more downstairs, fingers tangled in the loose threads of the couch, awake enough to know she was sleeping and didn't have to get up.

Somehow, the sleep lingered sweet even after she went back to school. It hurt to sit through class, hurt to use the toilet. But Jessie was happy. She didn't even care when a girl in the hall yelled, "Hey, how come you're walking like you've got an ear of corn stuck up your butt?"

Now she spent all her time trying to find that sleep again. In study hall she drifted beneath humming fluorescent lights. When Easy threw her it happened too fast to see or think or feel, but it unfolded now. The horse lifted her high until, as in dreams, gravity released her. Her legs floated up toward the arena ceiling, where summer after summer barn swallows nested. The reins tumbled from her fingers. Her face tilted down to Easy's neck. If she had an extra second she would kiss him goodbye.

Heavy hands landed on her shoulders. "Excuse me!" said the study-hall monitor. "No sleeping!"

No sleeping. Now was the time for reading. Hester Prynne, Pearl, some guys. Mom said school wasn't that important, it was just something they made you do, and when you're eighteen it's over. Which made Jessie suspect it was important, except she didn't understand how *The Scarlet Letter* was going to get her off the farm. Moreover, when she tried, really tried, stayed up until midnight doing homework, she got Cs in everything. When she didn't try, she got Cs in almost everything and had to stay after school for failing a math test.

The bell rang. Up the stairs, down the hall to sixth-period lunch. Jessie sat at the far end of the cafeteria, between the a la carte line and the boys' bathroom. At the next table, Angie Osuldsen and her volleyball teammates were in hysterics. They squeaked like Grandma's dogs, and sometimes Jessie couldn't stand it, how much she hated everyone.

"You know she's pregnant, right?" Elissa, Milo's owner, hitched a leg up over the bench. Elissa often joined her at lunch, and Jessie supposed they were friends, although Elissa made her desperately uncomfortable. She looked like a cartoon, like a doll, small everywhere except her wide blue eyes. Near her, Jessie was giant. Ugly. Near Elissa, Jessie reeked of horse manure.

"Who?" Jessie asked.

"Angie. In English everybody pretends they're talking about Hester Prynne, but they're really talking about her. She won't say whose it is. If it were me I'd run away up north until it was over."

"I don't understand why anyone would want to do it with a boy in the first place," Jessie mumbled. When Mom's boyfriend Terry was over he always sat around in his underwear and scratched his hairy stomach. When Mom and Terry did it, the walls rattled. Three years ago—the first time—Mom screamed, and Jessie ran through the house to Mom's room—it's happening, she thought—something is happening. Then Mom hit her hard on the side of the head, and now whenever Jessie said she didn't like Terry, Mom said, "Of course you like him," and talked about how Jessie's father used to whack Jessie across the backs of her knees with a riding crop.

* * *

That evening, Grandma, sitting in her recliner and holding a gray Chihuahua in her lap, watched TV in the living room. Jessie barely had time to drop her backpack before Terry walked out of the hallway bathroom with one hand down his pants. He fiddled around for a moment, twitched his left leg and then his right, grunted, and said, "She wants you in the barn."

"I haven't had my hot chocolate yet. Mom always lets me have hot chocolate first."

"Well I don't know what *Mom* always does but right now *Mom* wants you in the barn."

Jessie looked at Grandma, and Grandma said, "Don't look at me. I don't make the rules. I haven't made the rules in a long time."

Vans belonging to lesson riders' parents clustered in the drive. In the kennel, Grandma's dogs released long, thoughtful barks. *Haroo. Haroo.* Jessie walked behind the barn and up the hill to the haymow. She pushed a bale through an open hatch.

"Hey. You could kill somebody."

Jessie knelt at the edge of the hatch. Elissa stood beside the ladder, hands on her hips. "What are you doing?" she asked.

"Throwing the hay down."

"What's up there?"

"Hay."

Jessie pulled another bale toward the hatch, and Elissa said, "Wait."

Elissa climbed the ladder. Jessie wanted to push the bale down anyway and knock her off, because being friends at lunch didn't mean Elissa could just follow Jessie around at the barn. But it took a few seconds to think, to wonder if getting hit by a bale of hay really would kill somebody—it probably could kill Elissa, who was so tiny—and in that time Elissa made it up.

"This is cool," Elissa said.

"You can't be up here."

"Why not?" Elissa turned a circle. Red-orange light from the hatch sketched the edges of her boots. "I like this. If I lived here I'd set up a fort."

"How do you know you like it? You can't see anything."

"Maybe you can't see anything. I have really good eyes."

Jessie had made plenty of forts when she was small, right after deliveries, when bales were stacked ten high. When the hay was new, she'd stretched long in sweet golden rooms. Of course, the forts never lasted. Hay got delivered, more hay than she could ever imagine. Each time it seemed like it would last forever, but the horses always ate it, and snow fell and snow melted, and Jessie turned thirteen and started high school.

Elissa followed Jessie down the ladder. Terry, wearing rubber boots and a Carhartt duck jacket, as if he knew anything at all about farms, entered the barn. He blinked his red eyes and spit into his goatee. "You doing your chores? She doesn't want you messing around."

Elissa gripped Jessie's arm as he walked into the arena. "I hate that guy," she whispered. "He seems totally rapey."

Jessie felt suddenly shaky and stiff, as if she were looking down from an edge. As if she had never seen Elissa before. Elissa had started the school year with blue-green hair, but now her hair was black as her riding breeches and knee-high dressage boots. She wore a T-shirt with a drawing of a bear up on its hind legs, holding a rifle. *The Right to Arm Bears*, the shirt said.

Elissa whispered, "Don't worry, I won't let him rape you," in Jessie's ear.

She disappeared into Milo's stall. She liked to climb up on his back and take naps on top of him. Mom hated that but couldn't do anything about it since Elissa was a paying boarder whose dad made a lot of money shooting lasers into people's eyes.

*   *   *

Every day, together, they unpacked Elissa's complicated silver lunch box. Tiny compartments were labeled with their contents: *Five baby carrots. Twenty calories. Zero grams of fat.* Adopting a quick, nasal voice, Elissa mimicked her mother: "There is an epidemic of obesity in this country and if you want to hate me for helping you then that's frankly the least of my worries." Jessie stopped buying lunch tickets and instead used the money in the à la carte line, getting cookies for herself and frosted Long Johns for Elissa. Elissa would lick the frosting and groan, "Calories! I must have calories!"

In early November, Jessie told her about the hot summer day three years ago, when they gelded Easy. He had looked weirdly flat, splayed out unconscious in the pasture with his tongue lolling out of his mouth and two vets crouched by his butt. Eventually one of them stood, and in his triumphant bloody glove he held a slimy, gray-white egg with thin strands of tissue trailing off it. Jessie ran all the way back to the house, vomited outside the kitchen, and burst into tears. Grandma came out and said, "You'll have to get over it, Jessie. This is the way things are."

"Jesus Christ." Elissa licked frosting from her lips and pointed her long john straight up in the air. "Do they not get that we're kids? And maybe we don't have to see everything all the time?"

"I'm not a kid," Jessie said. "I'm basically just unpaid labor."

"Yeah but at least no one's watching you. The only reason Mom doesn't watch me at the barn is she thinks the barn is gross."

Elissa loved coming to the farm because that was the only time anybody left her alone. Otherwise she was at school, or at gymnastics practice, or doing crunches while her mom counted. Elissa's mom dropped her off most nights and often didn't come pick her up until after Jessie had gone inside for dinner. Still, Jessie had glimpsed her once or twice, and at least she was pretty, with jewels in her hair and painted nails and blood-red lipstick. Jessie's mom had papery skin, yellow teeth, and a thick mole under her eye.

"The barn is gross," Jessie said. "The house is gross too."

Elissa, with her big eyes, always seemed shocked, or at least intensely interested. She spoke with donut still in her mouth. "Do you want to come over? My house is a mansion, basically. Because of course her highness can't live in a normal house like normal people. I have a big room, and the closet is so big we call it the little room, and I have a daybed in there for sleepovers. You can come over on Friday, and then after the witch is asleep we can go on a pantry expedition."

In her afternoon classes, Jessie couldn't remember if Elissa had said that her bedroom and the little room were on the third floor of the mansion, and the little room had white walls and a slanted ceiling. If Elissa had told her, or if Jessie simply knew. On the bus ride home, in her mind, Jessie slept. Elissa's clothes, sweet as lilacs, hung protective in the pitch dark above. Not wanting to sleep alone,

Elissa slipped in beside her. Jessie stretched an arm and leg as far as she could but still didn't reach the edge of the daybed. Plenty of room for both of them, and hours of night still left.

That evening, during a lesson, she asked her mom, and Mom said no. Jessie had anticipated this and prepared her argument. "I'll get everything ready before I go. I'll clean all the saddles."

"Heels down!" Mom called to the lesson riders. "Straighten those shoulders." She rubbed her temple despairingly. "Jessica, why are you bothering me about this now?"

Jessie went to Milo's stall. "That's good," Elissa said. "She'll be thinking about it. What else can you offer?"

Jessie cringed. "The bathrooms, if I have to. I'm pretty sure there are rats in Grandma's bathroom and there's gunk in the toilets."

"Okay, well, see if the saddles are enough."

Elissa slipped down off Milo's back and followed Jessie to Easy's stall. Jessie clipped a longe line to his halter, and they walked out to the paddock. Jessie tapped Easy's shoulder with a whip and played the line out long. Elissa lit his great muscles with a flashlight, cast his shadow far into the weedy grass. "He's so pretty," she whispered.

"He's just showing off," Jessie said, but she was proud. Easy was good on the longe line, calm and supple, and her work had made him good. She clicked her tongue, and he picked up a trot. The line turned, taut in Jessie's hand and hotly bright under the flashlight. "It feels like you should be jumping over it," Jessie said.

"You think I can't?" Elissa dropped the flashlight and walked out between Jessie and the horse. Just as the line came around, she turned her back to it and launched into an arcing flip, so smooth and quick that Easy barely flicked an ear. She returned to the ground inverted, for an instant standing on her hands, and crouched low before the line circled again.

* * *

On Wednesday after school, Jessie put an English saddle on Easy. She practiced shoulder-ins at a trot, and Mom called,

"That's nice but you're using too much leg! Back off on the aid. He hears you."

The door at the far end of the arena eased open. A girl figure appeared and for a moment was shadowy, dim, as if darkness from outside still clung to her. As Jessie passed, the figure smiled bright and became Elissa. Jessie swung her hip to cue a canter. She rode Easy down the diagonal, tilted her weight, massaged the rein. He grunted and shifted his shoulders and floated into a half pass.

"Where did this come from!" Mom cried. "Who do you think you are?" But she laughed. She was pleased.

Jessie cantered the horse until he broke a lathered sweat and steamed in the cold. After Elissa slipped back out of the arena, she let the reins go long. Mom walked up to her and said, "Who is this horse? I've never seen this strong, obedient horse before." She squeezed Jessie's calf, just above her boot.

Jessie's blood rushed and warmed her. She couldn't stop her love for this asshole horse, and his muscles pulsing, and his tongue playing thoughtfully under the bit. She scratched between his ears. "He's good. He's a good horse."

They left the arena together, Jessie and Mom and Easy. Elissa hurried into the aisle and gripped Jessie's arm. "Come on, I need to show you something."

"I have to untack Easy."

But Mom, incredibly, took the reins and said, "I'll handle him. You go on."

Jessie followed Elissa up to the haymow. Elissa ran over bales as if on solid ground, quick and light, and Jessie, despite all her years in this barn, could not keep up. As Elissa ran toward a far starlit window, Jessie half-expected her to raise her arms and fly.

She disappeared. In an instant, she was gone, and empty bales stretched in every direction. Jessie wanted to scream but managed only to choke, "Elissa!" and scramble forward. If she found the fissure where Elissa had fallen, found it fast, then she could pull Elissa out before she suffocated.

"Hurry up!" Elissa called. A thin, dusty light shot up from the bales. Jessie hurried toward it and found Elissa in a cavern three bales deep. She'd jammed a flashlight into the hay and laid a blanket out. On top of the blanket, she set a box of crackers, a copy of *Seventeen*, a pack of cigarettes, and a bottle labeled Ron Rico.

"Now we have a fort!" Elissa said. "We can come up here whenever we need to escape."

"We can't smoke," Jessie said, because for once she didn't want the barn to burn.

"Maybe you can't. I've done it before." Elissa lit a cigarette, sat back against the hay, and inhaled with her eyes closed. She breathed a long trail of smoke to the rafters and said, "This is the life."

Jessie sat beside her and picked up the bottle. "It's alcohol?"

"Try it. It's good. My mom has it every night."

Jessie's eyes watered as soon as she unscrewed the cap. She tilted it to her lips anyway, and it burned, and she leaned coughing over the blanket. Elissa, laughing, drummed her fists on Jessie's back. "Not like that! You have to drink it and not think about it." She took a swig, swallowed hard, and grinned. "See? Easy," she said, but even in the weak light Jessie could see tears shining at the edges of Elissa's eyes. They made her smile, those sweet tears, and she tried again. This time the Ron Rico made it all the way down to the pit of her stomach and burned there steady.

Elissa said, "I wish we could just live here. It doesn't matter that it's cold."

Elissa shivered, and her breath puffed white in the dark. Jessie slipped an arm around her shoulders. "I don't think we should live here. I want to live at your house. I want to live in the little room."

"What! You haven't even seen it."

"I don't need to see it. I already know it's perfect."

"Well jeez. I don't want to just live in my own room. How about this. We can run away to my cabin up north. There's a wood burning stove and everything."

"That would be good. Let's do that." Elissa melted into Jessie's side, and suddenly, somehow, she didn't seem so small, and Jessie herself didn't feel so big. She tilted her head to smell Elissa's hair. "You can bring Milo and I'll bring Easy."

"Will you teach me to ride Easy?" Elissa whispered.

"Yes," Jessie whispered back. And she remembered her earliest days, when she and Mom would ride together. A pinto, bareback, Mom holding Jessie before her. They rode through the woods, over fallen logs, through laughing sunlit creeks. Jessie, not understanding how little she was, how meaningless, patted the horse's neck.

Jessie's hand moved down Elissa's shoulder, found space under her arm, felt the bird of her heart fluttering wild against the far wall of her chest. Elissa's breath pulsed faster, and all Jessie wanted in the world was to taste it. To hold it. She pressed her hand to Elissa's cheek and tilted her face up and it was happening, it was real, but Elissa got up so fast there was no time to think or feel or understand.

"I have to go."

"Your parents haven't come," Jessie said, and why would Elissa leave! But she darted like a barn cat back across the bales, back to the hatch glowing red. Jessie swallowed Ron Rico like water, then coughed and coughed until she collapsed across Elissa's blanket.

She crawled to the hatch and down the ladder. Elissa already had Milo in the crossties, saddled. A helmet shadowed her face. Mom pushed a broom down the aisle. "Go in and get dinner," Mom said. "It's getting late."

Elissa got up on a stool to unclip Milo's halter. Jessie couldn't breathe. She was going to throw up, she was going to wet herself, she was going to faint. She collapsed into Easy's stall, tangled her fist in his mane, and pressed her face into his withers because he was happy, eating from his manger, and his winter coat was thick as a teddy bear's.

"What are you doing?" Mom said. "He doesn't need anything. Go eat."

Jessie went straight to her room. She curled up in her narrow bed and tried to read *The Scarlet Letter*, fell asleep almost immediately, and dreamed she was still reading. She dreamed of blue sky untroubled around the little room. She loved Hester Prynne and felt love in return, pure as white walls, safe and warm as a daybed too big for one person.

From the way Hester Prynne was Elissa, and Elissa was Angie Osuldsen, the pregnant girl at school, Jessie knew she must be dreaming. In a dream she could hold onto an instant. And to the ends of Angie's hair. She could understand and explain. Without the lunch box, without you laughing, I can't take it, I can't think, I can't load horse manure into wheelbarrows. Without you the hay turns to great blocks of ice, and I try to climb until my fingers crack.

Her left foot worked its way out of the blanket and, cold, it woke her. The numbers on her clock radio glowed green. *9:17.* Jessie eased her door open and followed the sound of the television downstairs, past the stacked dishes in the kitchen sink, to the living room where Mom sat on Terry's lap, a blanket over their legs.

"Momma."

"Don't ask to change the channel. Terry wants to watch this."

"Mommy, can I please sleep over at Elissa's house on Friday?"

"What are you talking about? I already told you no."

"But if I clean all the saddles—"

"What do saddles have to do with anything?"

"I'll clean the bathrooms. I'll even do the toilets."

"Why do you have to spend the night with that girl? Don't you see her every day anyway? Because apparently if you're rich as stink you don't have to take care of your own kid, so I have to do it, because that sure is fair."

Jessie's throat tightened. Her words came out thin and high, more childish than she wanted. "Maybe I just want to because you never let me do anything."

"Good enough, little lady. Sounds like I'm just a monster."

Terry pointed the remote violently at the TV, tapping the volume up. "Any chance we can have it quiet long enough to watch this show?"

"Any chance you could stop being so rapey?" Jessie mumbled.

He lurched up, pushed Mom away, threw the remote to the floor. His eyes got big and veiny, and God, Elissa, you're so right, he's so incredibly rapey in his boxers and sweat-stained t-shirt. Flakes of dead skin in his ugly rapey mustache. Spit at the corners of his mouth.

"What the fuck did you say? What the fuck did you call me, you little slut?"

He slapped her air away, slapped her dizzy to her knees.

She raised a hand to her burning cheek. She believed for a second that Mom would chase Terry away. Son of a bitch.

"Will you come off it! She's just being an idiot! She's a kid and she's an idiot and that's all!" Mom kicked the blanket away, grabbed the remote. "Jessica, go to your room!"

"Her room?" Terry screamed. "That's all you're going to do?"

Fear and fury caught her as she ran for the stairs, and she burst into roaring sobs. She slammed her door, threw herself onto her rattling bed, and cried long and hard enough to drown out Mom and Terry and the television. The starless night pressed close to her window and seemed about to extinguish her lamp. Eventually the crack beneath her door went dark. The floor creaked heavily in the upstairs hall, and Terry said, "If she doesn't put a lid on it I'll break her teeth."

Weepy and weak, Jessie felt her way down to the kitchen, where the oven light blinked *11:04*. She took the phone from its cradle and couldn't quite decide if the long, lonely dial tone comforted or terrified her. She dialed, and after four rings Elissa, who had her own phone in her bedroom, answered.

"Mom said no about the sleepover," Jessie whispered, the phone heavy in her hand. "I said I'd clean the bathrooms and she still said no."

"Okay." Elissa sounded distant, fuzzy, her voice full of little holes.

"It's not fair. She never lets me do anything. I never even ask to do anything." She closed her eyes and clenched her teeth, trying to hold back the tears that welled once more in her chest. If only she were not so tired. If only the night didn't press so heavy on the ceiling tiles, and needles of hay weren't stuck in her jeans. If only it were lunchtime, and she and Elissa never ran out of things to say about their horrible, stupid mothers.

"I hate it," Jessie whispered, "and I'm scared. I'll never get out of here. She won't let me leave even for a night."

"Yeah well. I'm not sure what you want me to do about it. I've got my own problems."

Jessie's heart stopped. From somewhere out in the wooded cold she saw herself small and empty on the kitchen floor, the phone cord noosed around her wrist. She heard her voice say, "Okay. I guess I'll see you tomorrow in school then."

She hung up the phone, drew her knees in tight, and whimpered into her hands until she found her way back to her body. When she paused for breath, the whimpering went on without her. A dog with inky eyes sat before her on the linoleum. It yipped, raised a pleading paw, and trotted into the living room just as the television lit up the doorway.

Jessie followed. She sat on the couch and tucked the blanket around her, even though Terry's sweat was in it. On the screen three women sat in a row, smiling big and patting powder onto their faces. A phone number scrolled along the bottom of the screen. The camera panned to a rat-faced man who grinned in disbelief and said, "Your mother. Your sister. Your friend from down the block! Twenty years younger. Snap! Just like that."

Grandma sat in her chair, all her color washed away, white hair and dead pale skin, quilted nightgown down to her ankles. The dog circled three times and settled in her lap. She drank beer from a plastic cup. "I like to watch and wonder who would want these things," she said.

"I want it," Jessie answered.

"You don't need makeup. You're a child and you look fine."

A statue of a pink-cheeked girl and a fluffy sheep appeared on the screen, spinning slowly on a mirrored base. Four easy payments.

Limited edition with real quartz movement. At the bottom of the screen a phone number. A price.

"I want to sleep all day and sell things on TV all night."

Grandma muted the volume. "Oh, Jessica," she said. "We all want that."

CARRIE GRINSTEAD grew up in Wisconsin and now lives in Los Angeles with her partner, Daniel, and Pickle, their rat terrier. Her short stories have appeared in Tin House, Joyland, *and other journals. She is working on a novella and a story collection.*

Pilgrimage

Rebecca Gummere

I.

Things that collide:

1. Accelerated particles.

2. My infant son's small body and the sucking chasm of death.

3. Years of ordained ministry and my new agnostic state.

II.

It is the eve of my visit to CERN, the world-renowned particle physics research facility located on the outskirts of Geneva and home to the Large Hadron Collider. The LHC, a circular seventeen-mile-long record-setting particle accelerator, is buried one hundred meters beneath the surface along the border between Switzerland and France. It is here at CERN, the European Organization for Nuclear Research, that the Higgs boson, often referred to as the "God particle," was detected, the tentative but optimistic confirmation coming in July of 2012.

In the videotaped announcement the CERN auditorium erupts in enthusiastic applause. British physicist Peter Higgs, who half a century before had proposed the controversial idea, removes his glasses, acknowledges his colleagues' accolades with a nod of his snowy head, and wipes his eyes.

Discovery of the Higgs boson represents a significant piece to—and for many, the completion of—the Standard Model, often called "the theory of almost everything." According to the theory, the God Particle is what gives mass to all matter.

In truth, I have an inchworm's grasp of these experiments and their theories, but I keep going over the same material again and again, hoping I will catch a nanosecond's glimpse behind the veil.

I open my laptop and log onto the hotel's free Wi-Fi, and pull up the bookmarked Wikipedia page with the display of the Standard Model. I stare at the chart and recite the words again: leptons and quarks, neutrinos and bosons—and the forces that hold sway over matter's fundamental interactions—the strong force, the weak force, the electromagnetic force, and gravity.

Out to one side of the grid, floating in a little box by itself, is the Higgs.

III.

Some quantum fundamentals:

1. There is something called the *uncertainty principle* that says there is uncertainty built into certain measurements of certain particles at the quantum level.

2. There is also something called *nonlocality*, or what Einstein called "spooky action at a distance," an idea he detested. Nonlocality assumes particles are "entangled" in a mysterious relationship wherein what happens to one particle affects the other equally in an identical manner, regardless of their proximity.

3. When scientists decide on the assumption they start with, it is called the *ansatz*, which in German can mean "approach" or "beginning" or "attempt."

4. Some scientists assert that in the quantum universe, anything that can happen, does.

5. Thus I am drawn to a discipline I will never comprehend.

6. This is not the first time that has happened.

IV.

It is early September. Two days before I had taken the train from the small town of Cosne-sur-Loire in Central France up to Paris, then from Paris down to Geneva. That morning I got up early to pack and to tidy the studio flat I'd rented in the small medieval village of Sancerre, where I'd just completed a language immersion program. It was my first trip to France, and the weeks studying had been taxing but gratifying.

CERN tours are in such high demand that they are fully booked months in advance. I imagined all the other people—college students, Dan Brown enthusiasts, history buffs, well-to-do bankers, engineers, doctors, teachers, actual scientists. Would there be anyone else like me, someone looking for a key? A pattern? A reason? Some elegant design sturdy enough to account for not just the world's thickness but the world's sadness?

I had been trying to secure a reservation since before I left for France, but without success. Toward the end of my stay in Sancerre I sent a pleading email to someone in CERN Reception and was informed twelve slots would become available at 8:30 that Saturday morning for a tour the following week. I was advised to move quickly.

*   *   *

I rose early on Saturday, giving myself plenty of time to pack. At 8:20 I glanced out the flat's narrow window to see the taxi had already arrived. My iPad sat on the small kitchen table, the screen opened to the still-dormant CERN tour reservations page.

I took a break from scrubbing the bathroom sink at eight twenty-six and scurried out to the kitchen and hit refresh, reloading the page.

At eight twenty-eight I piled bed linens on the floor and ran back to hit refresh again. I sat down at the kitchen table, my eyes trained on the tablet's screen and hit refresh. It was eight twenty-nine.

I hit refresh again.

Then again.

And then it was eight thirty and the page opened to a blank reservation form. My hands shook as I typed in my information, begging the gods of Wi-Fi to hold the connection from the router that was buried somewhere within the sixteenth-century building on the other side of the cobblestoned street.

I hit *send* and a reply bounced back saying, *Thank you for your request.* No mention of when, or if, I would have an actual reservation.

I dragged my suitcase down the curve of narrow stone steps and out through the heavy door toward the waiting taxi.

*   *   *

Two hours later I sat on the grimy floor of Paris Gare de Lyon, tearing into a baguette stuffed with ham and butter, alternating with fistfuls of fresh juicy Mirabelle plums. A hot wind blew through the cavernous hall, mingling with sounds of traffic and the low chthonic rumble of arriving and departing trains.

I had bought my train ticket to Geneva, deciding even if I was not granted a coveted spot in a tour, I would by God go sit in the lobby. One way or another I was going to CERN.

V.

In 1986, four years after my son died, I entered seminary. I graduated in the summer of 1993 and was ordained two weeks later.

I remember kneeling on hard brick as the bishop placed his hands on my head. Behind me, several other pastors stepped forward, placing their hands on my shoulders and back, until I felt I might collapse beneath the accumulating weight.

> **BISHOP.** Before almighty God, to whom you must give account, and in the presence of this assembly, I ask, Will you assume this office, believing that the church's call is God's call to the ministry of word and sacrament?
> **ME.** I will, and I ask God to help and guide me.
> **BISHOP.** Will you give faithful witness in the world, that God's love may be known in all that you do?
> **ME.** I will, and I ask God to help and guide me.

Eight years after leaving the church, my many-colored liturgical stoles and faded robe still hang in a far corner of my closet, as if I am a jilted bride.

VI.

The sky was covered over with clouds as we pulled out of the Gare de Lyon. The young woman seated next to me flirted with the young man across from her. Soon they disappeared in the direction of the bar car. We would be three-and-a-half hours flying across the rails to Geneva. The landscape slid by in a long colorful blur, and I nodded off to sleep.

* * *

Upon our approach into Geneva the train slowed and then lurched, and I came around to see sudden tall rocks jutting on either side of the railway and the bright blue of opening skies as the late afternoon sun burned and melted through the clouds. The young woman and her new friend returned to their seats, the perfume of hot skin radiating from their bodies.

Outside the sprawling Geneva Cornavin complex, I waved toward a long line of taxis, and one moved forward to meet me. The driver was from Spain. He did not speak English, and I don't speak Spanish, so we each used our own form of halting French and managed to carry on a simple but brief conversation.

"He likes it here."

"I am tired from my trip."

"Geneva is very nice."

Inside the Swiss-themed hotel stenciled flowers bloomed on every inch of available wood, and accordion music floated out from the dining room. After checking in, I pulled my suitcase into the tiny elevator and rode upstairs to my room, where I collapsed onto the bed and lay on my back staring at the ceiling. The folly of what I had done washed over me in a sick rush.

What in God's name was I doing here? Did I even know?

VII.

Things you probably should not confess to your seminary professor:

1. I believe the future is not fixed but is open-ended, infinite with possibility.

2. I believe even God does not know what is going to happen next.

3. I believe God is continually creating the world, including this moment and the next and the next, and that God's own self is eternally "becoming."

* * *

"That is called process theology," my instructor had grumbled, his gray beard stiff with indignation.

(Thus I was in trouble from the beginning.)

"Well, I think that's what I believe."

(What did I have to lose, really?)

"You probably don't want to tell that to too many people."

(He was probably right on that point.)

"But what about the terrible suffering that people endure?" I pushed. "Am I supposed to accept that it is all 'part of God's plan?' What kind of God allows that? And what if there is no plan?"

(In those moments, I believed my theological stance provided an escape clause for God's culpability.)

"Faith," he likely would have said, "in things unseen."

VIII.

Later, friends back home will ask me about my time in Geneva. Some had traveled here, some attended university, others had come to live and work, but the embarrassing truth is, I mostly lay around the hotel room playing solitaire on my iPad, reading *The Martian*, and taking short naps.

When I went out at all I kept a tight perimeter around the hotel. I wandered in and out of shops, and spent too much money on a jar of skin cream I would later throw out because I could not abide the sickening sweet smell. I ate hurried lunches and dinners at outdoor cafes. A couple of times I wandered out to sit by the lake to watch the tossing waves and listen to the metallic clang of rigging on sailboat masts. I could see the bridge to the famed Old Town, with its picturesque shops and narrow streets, but I did not go there.

On my second day in Geneva I received an email confirming my reservation for an upcoming tour in two days.

IX.

It is now late at night, and the sounds of reggae-rap fusion rise from the plaza below where people are singing and dancing. I watch for a moment, feeling both envy and frustration. A wild part of me wants to run outside and join them, but I need sleep. Even though the room is stuffy and the clean night air feels good, I shut the window.

"Tomorrow I am going to CERN," I say out loud, and climb into bed, punching the lumpy pillow to reshape it. When I do finally sleep I dream that as I exit the tram I see a former husband walking with a group of scientists. He is talking and laughing, and everyone's eyes are fixed on him. I feel somehow betrayed and cannot figure out why he is there at all.

I wake too early and eat breakfast too fast—the coffee is flavorless and the bowl of muesli resembles chopped twine topped with thin chalky yogurt. Back in my room, I try to write down my thoughts but I cannot focus. I am anxious I won't find the right tram, anxious even if I do, I might somehow miss the stop for CERN. I decide I can be anxious in the reception area at CERN just as easily as in my hotel room that is beginning to annoy me with its persistently cheerful alpine motif.

I walk the several blocks to the train station, and join a misshapen clump of people waiting for tram number eighteen. I stand off to one side, wondering at the start of tears, wondering exactly what weight I have asked this journey to carry. What revelation did I seek? What revelation would suffice?

X.

An elderly woman boards the tram and the dark-haired woman next to me stands and offers her seat. The elderly woman leans heavily on her cane and lowers her body onto the narrow bench.

She smells of soap and perfume and warm perspiration. She smiles sweetly and speaks to me in French. I nod, catching a little of what she is saying.

"She hurts. It is difficult."

Then with a shrug she tells me, *Ce n'est pas grave.* "No matter."

When her stop comes up, her knees will not cooperate, and my hand goes to her back as she tries to stand.

It is an automatic gesture. My mother is dead and gone to ash for eighteen months now, but my hand does not remember that.

The wool of the woman's coat is soft under my fingers. She thanks me, offers a sweet smile, and then exits. As the tram pulls away I begin to weep, turning my face to the window. So many gone now. Mother, father, sister, son.

I cry all the way to the end of the line, to CERN.

*   *   *

Last night in my dream I had seen a different place entirely, like something out of a Bond movie, with tall gleaming stainless steel and stark concrete and an M. C. Escher–like series of levels and stairways.

Instead, low-lying buildings sprawl across either side of the street, nondescript and unremarkable. In the distance, the heavily forested Jura Mountains ripple in the midmorning sun.

It is hard to believe I am here. Something feels flat and unreal, even unnecessary. I pull out my cell phone and take a photo of the street sign that says CERN. Who will care about this picture? I wonder, even as I am taking it.

In front of me is a pile of tattered blankets on a slatted metal bench, clumps of matted gray hair and beard protruding from one end, and I have a wild thought that any moment a fairy tale wizard in a star-covered cloak will throw off the blanket and stand, brandishing a staff.

Clearly, I am expecting magic, a sad habit I am trying to shake.

Beneath the homeless man are a crumpled paper bag and wadded-up food wrappers, and the entire area reeks of urine and cigarettes. After a moment, I follow the group of people into the crosswalk, heading toward CERN Reception. I do not look back at the pile of blankets.

I am so early that I'm the first one to check in. A pretty blond woman who speaks English with a thick accent gives me my visitor's badge and points to a door next to a coffee machine. There, she tells me, is where I am to be exactly five minutes before the tour is to start. In the meantime, I can visit the display that is downstairs.

Embedded in the floor in the center of the entryway is an art installation, "Cosmic Song," which is actually a cosmic-ray detector. Brass and steel plates interweave with kaleidoscopic runnels of colored lights, lines and curves and bends and swirls reminiscent of Aztec artwork. I stand in the middle of the flickering lights for a moment, then follow signs, past newly renovated walls dotted with fresh plaster, down a long ramp to the small display. The end wall is entirely covered with an enormous photograph of the mouth of the Hadron, which from far away looks like a starfish, or a spider, or a nerve ending.

I take a series of out of focus pictures with my cell phone because I have come all this way and I think I should, but my heart is really not in it, my mind going back to the man sleeping on the bench.

Back upstairs I pace, loiter, sit, pace some more, and finally go to the small gift shop next to the reception area. There are t-shirts, plastic hard hats, pens, jackets, all bearing the CERN logo, and three tables stacked with books about quantum physics, particles, and the facility's history, in English, French, and German. I buy two books, one a short introduction to particle physics and the other about neutrinos. I will add these to my small library at home, so that I will have a collection of more books I don't fully comprehend.

I find a wall to lean against and wait.

XI.

I am rocking my six-week-old son, listening to the low creak of the old chair. He has been sick, and he is so quiet now.

Correction: he had surgery and then we brought him home and now he is sick, and too quiet.

Actually: he was born with a heart defect and had heart surgery and then came home and was doing better and gaining weight and beginning to notice his big brother with dark-eyed interest and to smile, but now he is sick, vomiting all day, and I took him to the pediatrician and gave him fluids and put him in a warm bath and swaddled him so that he finally stopped wailing, but now—now he is so quiet, and some eely thing inside me begins to move toward the surface, but I don't want to know, I don't want to know.

Later, I will keen over the shell of his small body, wondering over and over: where had he gone?

XII.

As the time draws near for the tour to begin a small crowd gathers by the coffee machine. When the room opens, we move in and take our seats. In front of us is a large screen.

I look around. People speak in hushed tones. A few sit staring at the floor, arms crossed. Others look around, eyes wide. I discover I am near tears again.

Our tour guide, a physicist, is a tiny Italian woman with short dark hair and darting eyes. She shows us a short introductory video. The accompanying music and cheerful graphics, along with the tone of the narrator's voice, all combine to give me the feeling of being back in school in my fourth-grade classroom at Bearden Elementary in Knoxville, Tennessee.

At the conclusion of the film she gives a brief speech about the origins of CERN, how it began in 1952, the same year I was born, as a consortium of European countries still reeling in the aftermath of World War II. Together they made a commitment to openness and transparency. Whatever is discovered belongs to the whole world, she tells us with pride.

"Take lots of pictures!" she urges, and the tour begins.

Because the LHC is currently online, public tours of the collider are not permitted, so our tour will be all above ground. I try to tamp down my disappointment, remembering I am lucky to be here.

We enter a building with an enormous glass wall, on the other side of which are about fifty people scattered across the room, sitting in front of computer screens. "This is the ATLAS control room," our guide tells us.

ATLAS stands for "A Toroidal LHC ApparatuS." (*Toroidal* means "donut-shaped," she says.) Currently the ATLAS experiment is looking for clues about dark matter, which is theorized to make up most of the universe and about which nothing is actually known.

We peer into the control room where dozens of flat screens display the day's activities and announcements. Up on the wall to the right are several large displays showing sparky renderings of ongoing events, proton collisions happening right now resulting in the creation of new particles that leave brightly colored trails like fireworks in a night sky. The collected information is being shared with thousands of scientists globally via the World Wide Web, which was created here at CERN for the sole purpose of maximizing the number of eyes on any given set of data.

We exit the building and cross back to the other side of the complex and walk through a doorway into a darkened room that houses the original "atom smasher," the Synchrotron. On a metal desk is an original computer that looks like a combination adding machine and typewriter. On the blackboard above the desk are several chalked equations and a *yes!* scrawled next to them. These marks are not original, our guide informs us with a smile.

She pauses so we can take pictures, and I begin to ask questions.

Why is the LHC so large? What is the purpose for its curved structure? Why hydrogen protons? I am wishing, along with everyone else in the tour group, that I would shut up, but I cannot seem to. I am trying to make some sort of connection here, feeling increasingly anxious, as if I'm moving invisible pieces around an invisible board with higher and higher stakes.

The tour guide describes again the purpose for the collider, which is one of the few things I do understand.

"What about the *ansatz*?" I ask.

"The what?" She peers at me.

Shut up shut up shut up.

"The assumption. The starting place."

"Yes," she says as if I am a tiresome child, and repeats again basic information about the collider, as if saying, "When a mommy proton and a daddy proton love each other very much . . . "

I lean back against the railing, the Synchrotron behind me. I feel chastised, shamed, and then stupid for feeling chastised and shamed.

I am not a scientist. I am just a woman looking for some goddamn answers.

XIII.

Ansatz #1: What if there is no God?
Ansatz #2: What if there is?

XIV.

What I have been suppressing all week: recently published pictures of dead Syrian toddlers washed up on the Turkish shore that is strewn with their small shoes; the sad careful way a Turkish officer cradles the body of a four-year-old boy.

XV.

We are back inside Reception now.

"This concludes the tour," says the smiling Italian physicist, and the group disperses and scatters. I stand in the lobby area, not sure what to do next. The cosmic detector glows, flashes, sparks.

At last I push through the gleaming double doors and out into the bright afternoon.

XVI.

I have fifteen euros in my pocket and decide I will give them to the homeless man, a sin offering for having ignored him earlier, but when I arrive at the tram stop he has vanished. Gone are the blankets, the food wrappers. Gone is the smell of piss and body odor and stale cigarettes.

It is as if he was never really there at all, and for just a moment I wonder if I might have imagined the whole thing.

REBECCA GUMMERE's work has appeared in The Gettysburg Review, The Rumpus, the New South Journal, O, The Oprah Magazine, *and other publications. She is a two-time Pushcart nominee, received a Fellowship from the Virginia Center for the Creative Arts, and was awarded a 2017–2018 North Carolina Artist Fellowship for her memoir-in-progress about her recent spiritual journey "Chasing Light," a nine-month cross-country trip in a small RV with two large dogs and not enough books.*

Rebecca has taught at Appalachian State University, worked for a domestic violence/rape crisis agency, and in another life served three Lutheran pastorates. She holds a BA from Wittenberg University, an M.Div. from Trinity Lutheran Seminary, and an MFA from Queens University of Charlotte. When not on the road, she lives and writes in the beautiful Blue Ridge Mountains of North Carolina, where she is involved in efforts addressing food equality and sustainability

Ghost Print

Anna Reeser

Walking to the studio that day, sun dripping thick between your eyelashes, you don't feel as painfully young as you are. Twenty-two, unshaven, hamburger in your back molars, and a hunger still there, still hovering in your blood. On the lawn, a girl's tan back is exposed, shoulder blades casting shadows, and if you pressed your palm to that skin, it would be hot to the touch.

Advanced printmaking students can use the press on Sundays, when campus is slow and dehydrated. You have a plate ready to print, and you hope Arielle will be in the studio, saying *hello*, confirming that you hadn't been an asshole last weekend. The stairs echo under your sneakers, and you key into the studio, meet the cool air face-first, the tang of ink. The etching press is a heavy, quiet beast that you've learned to tame. Eleanor and Jack are there, eating sub sandwiches at the worktable, pieces of lettuce falling by their etching plates.

"Hey Charlie." Eleanor barely looks up, wire-rimmed glasses midslide down her nose, a billowing yellow shirt from the eighties. *Charles* was how you signed prints now, how you titled your CV for grad-school applications, but it isn't worth saying. Eleanor adds, "Mike's in the acid room. Professor Ellis gave him the codes."

"Why the hell?" It should be you entrusted with the codes, submerging your plates on weekends, watching bubbles form on the exposed zinc, the metal corroding away.

"He's a forty-year-old undergrad," says Jack. "Ellis wants him to feel less lame."

Mike emerges from the acid room in a yellow smock, protective goggles on his face.

"Hey, man," you say. "Biting some metal?" You make the sign of the horns and instantly regret mocking him.

Then the room cracks open with sound, a gasp-scream that sucks all the air out. Eleanor drops her sandwich, hands trembling, eyes wide over her phone. "Oh, God—Jack—oh *God*."

"What?"

"Arielle."

"Let me guess, she joined that freakshow co-op. She threatened to. It's *vegan*, so."

"No—fuck—Jack, *shut up*—she died."

"What?"

"It's a—a fucking—department email." Eleanor's eyes are wide and dry, her voice halts, angry, choking, but not crying. "Car accident on Highway 1."

You feel hollowed out, brain desiccated. Your tongue flops against your teeth and you sit on a metal chair, hands steadying on the table. There is nothing to say. Your first thought is that you have not experienced a death before—your grandparents are still alive. Then you think of her, of her face in the porchlight, how she kept making eye contact. You are terrible, and pain hits your gut like an etching needle jabbed under the skin.

"It was last weekend. Jesus. She wasn't in studio Wednesday."

"Read the email." Jack peers over Eleanor's shoulder at the phone.

"No."

"I'll read it. *It is with great sadness that we inform you of the unexpected loss . . .*"

"Stop," says Mike. "Not out loud." He stands by the table, taking off his goggles. Underneath, his eyes are glazed, his face is red and sweaty. He softly removes his rubber gloves and rubs his calloused hands together. He looks briefly up at the ceiling, then turns and leaves, not even taking off the yellow smock, and the door thunders behind him.

"I think he has a kid," says Jack. "Makes people sentimental."

"Will you shut up?" Eleanor cradles her face in her hands.

* * *

The first time you saw Arielle outside of class was last Friday. A house party in Oakland that had drifted into the backyard, light spilling out the open door. Still cold, everyone gripping their jacket sleeves, cigarettes between shivering fingers. "Like a little campfire," you heard Arielle say across the porch. A guy—mousy but older, maybe a grad student—held out the light for her, his hand close to her face, her lips.

You walked by to get in line for the keg, a satisfying compound of alcohols under your skull, a sloshing boat-like feeling, and Arielle's eyes darted out at you, like she needed something to hold onto.

"Charlie!"

You stopped, she orbited you, and her skin in the light looked like milk. A thin face, ringed with rust tendrils, even redder in the porchlight. She looked like a Dutch portrait, something expansive about her forehead. She turned halfway to the guy and said, "He's in my printmaking class," and then she fixed on you.

She wore a red flannel shirt with the top four buttons undone. The fabric looked soft against her chest. She asked if you'd started your aquatint, and you said you had.

"I don't know how I feel about mine," she said. "On one hand, you get this amazing tonal range. But it's hard to translate the original image though the process."

You smirked at her—using the phrase *tonal range* on a Friday night. But it was gorgeous, the way she talked, and you nodded on.

"But there is something that I like. My image never comes out exactly, and by now I know it's never going to come out exactly, so I'm more forgiving about how it looks. It's like, at least it printed. Whatever prints, I kind of accept it. I kind of love it."

It made sense that she'd think that; her prints were always a mess, semiabstract, with some figure in a corner with badly drawn hands. Like Chagall, maybe. You'd use the word whimsical. It wasn't your thing—you were a formalist, a drafter of cow skulls or glass jars—you'd say art was about taking a challenging subject in a challenging medium and executing it with astonishing skill. Why else use the methods? Why else stand in the acid room brushing bubbles off the plate with a feather, why else rub ink onto metal with a grimy wad of tarlatan? "I mean sure, but the point is the technique," you said. "Getting the best possible result. Otherwise, is it worth *etching*?"

"Sure, I get that," she said, a dip in her voice. But she brightened again, stepped closer. Slid her hands into the back pockets of her jeans. "Ellis is so great, right? Such a jovial tyrant. Definitely a reason to be in printmaking."

"Hell yeah, team Ellis," you said, a mocking voice ballooning out of your mouth, even though you agreed, absolutely agreed, the rigidity of Ellis's studio was great. It was a secret society, an esoteric body of knowledge shared by few. But it was weird to see each other outside the studio like this, drunk in a feral backyard. You were horny, she was eloquent.

"I'm curious about your work," Arielle said. "Why do you draw still lives; what's the most interesting part for you?" There was no snark, no jab—she just asked the question. You stared blankly for a second. *Why?* It was Friday night, you weren't answering that. What was this, critique? Nobody asked why, not even Ellis. The guy still hovered nearby and seemed to be eyeing you weirdly, a step-off thing. He could be her boyfriend, what did you know. Your housemates caroused in a corner of the yard and a swarm of girls crowded onto a sagging hammock. Arielle's earnestness frightened you, the way she made eye contact, as if she saw something in you that you couldn't live up to.

You mumbled that you had to go, then walked away abruptly, to the keg line, and from there you watched her. The curve of her neck, her pensive downcast eyes. Her leather boot tapping. You would like to date her, theoretically, to undress her. But she was so thoughtful, too thoughtful, someone you'd like to date in ten years, when your work was recognized, when you had three to five gray hairs, when you'd already fucked around. From the keg line, you saw the guy move in, speak close to her face. Boyfriend. Then, you saw it like a film—flat and washed out by the porchlight. She looked back—for you? Was it panic, or just the cold, the sickening taste of cigarettes? A hand on her hip, leading her through the side gate, the revving of an antique-sounding engine, and gone.

It could have been that night, that car. She had looked back— had she wanted an exit route? If you'd talked to her for ten, twenty minutes, she wouldn't have gone wherever she went.

*   *   *

Light dims and thickens to ochre through the studio windows. Eleanor paces, then her fingers drift across the flat file drawer with Arielle's name in block letters on a piece of masking tape. Jack comes up behind her and hugs her shoulders, kisses her ear. They were a couple when they started the class, together since sophomore year, incredibly.

Jack opens the drawer full of Arielle's prints and plates.

"What are you doing?" says Eleanor. "Close it. *Close it.* That's her stuff." Her voice is full, like she wants to cry but somehow can't.

"You guys weren't even friends."

"We *were.*"

"Come on, you never hung out. Name one time."

"She was here. She was in the studio. She ate almond-butter sandwiches right there, right at that seat. Right, Charlie?"

"Yeah." Your voice cracks badly. Her sandwiches always looked good, and you'd once told her that, and she offered you a half. You smirked and said *no thanks*, but you had wanted nothing more than the tack of almond butter on the roof of your mouth, cut with blueberry jam.

"She made that print of a window, a tree through a window," says Eleanor.

"Look, here's one of them." Jack reaches for a sheet in the drawer, but Eleanor slaps his hand away.

"I need some air," she says, firm and sharp, then rustles out and slams the door.

Jack looks at you and shakes his head. "Heavy shit." You nod. He gathers the remains of their sandwiches and throws them away. Shrugging exaggeratedly, he backs toward the door. "Later, man. I better go talk to her."

The studio is deeply quiet, and you pace around the table to hear your footsteps. Twirl an etching needle in your hand, the weight of it, the sharp point. Open your flat file drawer, stare at the plate that you were ready to ink and print. It's a still life of etching tools—needles, burnisher, a jar of stop-out varnish—rendered precisely in crisp lines and shadows modulated by the tonal range of the aquatint process. Classical realism. The kind of work you'd assumed you should make if you were technically capable. As if this ability made you an artist. When it's inked and printed, the objects will appear to be sitting on the paper. But why? The needles and burnisher and jar already exist.

You close your drawer and open Arielle's, thickness building in your throat. Stacks of paper, hastily printed, some with smudges of inky fingers on the white border. There are figures, but obscured—the idea of a hand, maybe a shoulder, an eye. Some prints you haven't even seen in critique. A new plate, eight by ten inches, shows a woman's figure in profile—almost a likeness of her. Behind the figure are tangled lines of hair, in front are tangled lines of rain. Or just lines. In the light, the etched lines are bright and shimmering.

Your heartbeat gets loud and weird, your mouth is still dry. There are sheets of paper soaking in the tray already, probably Eleanor's. The press, the monolithic thing, seems to watch you as you spin its cranks to lower the roller and adjust the layers of padding. Presses like this are rare, hidden in university art departments, in the garages of a few masters. You spread ink on a sheet of plexiglass and work it back and forth with a palette knife until it's glossy as the ocean in moonlight.

Off Highway 1. You picture the curving road, a chaos of red and metal, then try not to. You picture her on the porch, her fringes of hair in the light, then try not to. At the party, after you walked to the keg line, you'd pictured meeting a version of her at NYU, where you would presumably be in graduate school, in the middle of a serious winter, in a larger version of the Berkeley studio. You had actually formed the thought, There will be Arielles in New York.

Part of you feels nauseous, but the ink is ready. This is why you came here, to print your new plate, to lay the prints carefully on blotting paper, to leave no smudges on the edges, to send these flawless images in your NYU application, to stay suspended in obsolete technology and terms, in this silo sealed off from the rest of the world.

You smear ink over your plate and, hand in a rubber glove, work it into the grooves with tarlatan. Filled with ink, your lines appear, rigid and unflinching. Hard shadows. No trace of your hand drawing. You hate it a little, there's something safe and fake about it—it doesn't move, it doesn't speak.

Hands sweating in the gloves, sweat building on your hairline. Your hair is too long, inching over your ears, and you've never had a girlfriend for more than two months. Your scalp itches, your back itches, your throat feels full of phlegm or tears. You should never have dismissed her. Setting your plate on the table, hands clumsy in the gloves, you grab Arielle's eight-by-ten. Maybe she would have been printing it today. The edge is sharp, just slightly beveled, and it digs a little into your thumb. For a second you pause, wondering if this is wrong, then you spread a gloss of ink onto the surface. You work it into the lines, scrubbing hard. After wiping the excess ink away, her image is stark on the metal. Chin curve, shoulder curve, hip curve, lines drawn by hand. A figure loosely rendered. Lines sometimes delicate and frantic, sometimes strong and crosshatched. It feels like movement and thought.

Snap out of it. Paper is getting waterlogged in the soaking tray. Put the plate on the press bed, and this time you don't spend minutes setting it perfectly on the aligning grid. Wash hands, lift out a hydrated sheet of heavy paper, blot so it's just damp, lay the paper on the plate fast, then the wool press blankets, and roll it through with hard heavy cranks. The light is low, peeking magenta through the window. When you peel the paper back, you hold your breath. It printed, at least it printed. The ink was laid too thick, and it's smudged in places, but the lines are visible through a scrim of plate tone. You picture Arielle looking at the print, then try not to.

Setting the print in your drawer between blotting papers, you almost gear up to reink, but then figure it's still got ink in the grooves—you might as well pull another one. A ghost print is what Ellis calls it, a second impression. So, you prepare another sheet and lay it on the plate, gently but without hesitating. You crank the pressure up one notch, and then roll it through slowly, so that every one of your muscles feels it.

This print is different—some lines are wispy and others loud, dancing on the paper. It's beautiful. Almost like it was just drawn in pencil, along to music, to a song that builds in pace and volume. You picture her drawing it in her bedroom with sound reverberating against the walls, then try not to.

Maybe in ten years, you will be making abstract etchings. The spare room in your apartment will be crowded with plates, ink-smeared gloves, a table top press that's finicky but prints. Window cracked open to the chill when the air gets thick with ink. Still using zinc plates, but drypoint—scratching right into the metal with a needle. No acid baths, no reference material, just the sound of the radio against the walls. The lines fine and quick with muscle or slow with a feeling you keep trying to get right. The feeling of heaviness in your chest, then an overwhelming fullness, the relief of a big breath. Sometimes the prints will come out, sometimes they won't. Really, there will be a thousand other things that never get captured, let alone etched, let alone printed—the way your girlfriend looks at you while you're watching TV, the light on her nose. In bed in the morning, pressing her face against your shoulder. There will be a night when you argue, and she slams the door, and you walk out in the cold, too, just to feel the same awful air, then you feel both vulnerable and whole seeing her walk back in the gold-blurred streetlight, and maybe soon after that, you'll get married. Your old prints will be in a black folio, all that paper together, three inches thick with the ghost print pressed inside, and it will have traveled from apartment to apartment, leaning against every off-white wall, soft dust clinging to the deckled edge.

The sun is so low that all you can see is a streak of red between two buildings. The window is open to the cooling air and the rushing sounds of cars on Bancroft Avenue. The studio feels as permeable as any other place. You set the print between your blotting papers and wipe down the plate with a rag. Wipe the press bed and slowly clean the inking station, wiping the plexiglass surface again and again. Loosen the pressure on the press, remove the blankets from under the roller and fold them in thirds. You put Arielle's plate back in her drawer and close it softly. You sit at the table for a while, until it's so dark you can't really see anything, and instead of turning on the lights, you just head out, fumbling past the table and the chairs and the press in the dark.

ANNA REESER's short fiction appears in The Nervous Breakdown *and* The Destroyer. *She was a recipient of the Dorothy Rosenberg Memorial Prize in Lyric Poetry, and her artwork has been featured on the cover of* CutBank. *Originally from Ojai, California, she holds a degree in English and Art Practice from UC Berkeley. Now based in the Pacific Northwest, she is writing a collection of short stories and works as a graphic designer. Find more of her work at annareeser.com.*

Rogue Particles

Laura Demers

E ve has been posting on Facebook that people are trying to ruin her. It seems plausible to me, as Eve was always so beautiful, a target for envy. She was even in *Vogue* once, eighteen years ago. A full-page photo of her and her sister, the sister in profile, Eve full faced, seaweed green eyes wide with empty wonder, cheekbones like a Slav, the small delicate chin. Now she is living in Brooklyn, working at an art gallery.

Fired today. Apparently I am a schizo.

This gets eighteen *likes*, giving the impression that people like that she has been fired. Underneath, however, are a couple of empathetic comments.

Don't worry, Eve. You will always end up on top! and, *Oh, no! Call my brother. He's in Manhattan now.*

I wonder what this brother will do for Eve. It goes quiet on Eve's Facebook page for weeks. When I check again, I see that only people wishing her a *happy birthday* have posted. *Hey, beautiful. Happy Birthday!* say the ones from men. *Happy Birthday, sweetie!* is typical of the women. But Eve does not respond, or even *like* these comments.

And then suddenly she writes, *Whoever is talking about me, spreading rumors about me, please stop.*

I feel a pang of guilt. I've checked Eve's page on and off for months now, ever since I finally succumbed to Facebook. I added Eve as a friend, and Eve wrote, *Hey, where have you been* and nothing more. This is a relief, as I don't want a real correspondence, any real type of contact. Eve was so draining, so full of drama. I prefer watching Eve's life from a distance. I long ago defected from the world we both inhabited. I was a stylist's assistant in my former life, to a successful stylist, who eventually fired me after giving me chance after chance. Now I'm a makeup artist on the opposite coast. I've even done a couple of celebrities for events. An actress from *The Walking Dead* and two reality stars.

It was actually Eve who helped me learn about makeup, long ago when we were teenagers. Eve helped me apply my foundation with a sponge, showed me how to do a cat's eye. I would never use these techniques now, but I still think of Eve's sure hand, even at fourteen, how she could make herself look seven years older, how she glittered under club lights.

Can you call me? Eve asks me in a message on Facebook. *What's your number?*

These two questions sum up most of Eve's problems. Never thinking in a cohesive way.

I ignore both questions for several days and then I get another message.

Are you in LA? I'll be in Santa Barbara maybe.

This is too close for me. Although I like Santa Barbara and imagine Eve's Santa Barbara to be fairly glamorous. I picture Eve staying with friends in a large gleaming house with a pool, maybe on the edge or even in Montecito.

Oh how great, I respond with some trepidation three days later. *When?*

I don't know exactly.

There are no more messages, but plenty of posts on Facebook. *Who is spreading these lies about me?* she writes. *Seriously. It started as gossip, but now it feels like people I don't even know are saying these things.*

I stop looking at Eve's profile. I can't decide what draws me to it, anyway, whether it's the glossy shots of Eve from twenty years before, in an ad campaign for Tommy Hilfiger, at a launch party for another clothing line with a famous actor from the nineties. Or the more current selfies, her features still delicate, her makeup still perfect, her hair maybe a bit thinner, her eyes sadder, her mouth tight in a grimace of unease. Eve was never meant to photograph herself. She is from the last generation that only had their picture taken by whoever was on hand: a parent, a boyfriend, in her case a famous photographer.

One day I get a phone call. It's an unknown number, so I let it go to voicemail. When I listen to it, I am amazed to hear Eve's voice, exactly as I remember it.

"I got your number from Alex. I ran into him in Brooklyn. He said he sees you sometimes."

I don't call back. Hours later I receive a text. *I'm in Santa Barbara.*

My heart gives a sick thud.

What are you doing there? I text back.

Can you call me?

I stare at the message. While I'm deciding what to do, Eve writes, *I'm in a sober house.*

*   *   *

Google Maps tells me to get off on exit 96B. I feel a flutter of nerves. I realize that one of the things I'm afraid of is what Eve will look like. Eve is one of those people who is meant to be beautiful, may not survive without it. While I'm reassured by the selfies she has posted, there are bound to be changes. There are women I'm happy to see age. Unkind women, dismissive women, the girls in New York who looked right through you if you couldn't help them. As a stylist's assistant, I had to deal with a lot of these types.

Eve was never one of them. Eve was never earthy or low-maintenance or easygoing. None of the things that make a woman forgive another woman for being lovely. She only had vulnerability. She was fragile, always in crisis, tormented by the day-to-day struggle of life. Her one gift was pulling it all together by night so that she could go out into it, cut through it like a shard of glass, refracting the light of the city back to it. I could never reconcile the tortured, frustrated girl on the phone with the one I would pick up in a cab an hour later. This second girl would appear like a pretty ghost, from the flapper era maybe, in a shimmery silk shift and high-heeled strappy shoes and a coat trimmed in ostrich feathers.

"We're meeting my friend Peter," she would say as she got in. "He got our names on the list."

Now I find the address on Victoria Street. I park around the corner, to give myself more time. I'm always trying to postpone life for another ten minutes, another twenty if I can. It used to cost me jobs. But I'm not ready for Eve. I flip down the visor and check my own face in its small mirror.

I'm older, too, of course. Fine lines between my eyebrows, bags underneath my eyes that never go away even when I've had eight hours of sleep, a narrowing at the temples, a faint sagging at the jaw. But otherwise, the same face, for the most part. I didn't have as much to lose as Eve. I remember a time at a nightclub on Lafayette when a table full of Italian men beckoned me over. I took a long sip of my drink and approached them.

"Who is your friend?" they asked.

They pointed to Eve, behind me, shimmering and bored. I kept my smile frozen in place and returned to the table.

"What did they want?" asked Eve.

"Nothing," I said. "They're idiots."

"You should have made them come to you."

Now, as I get out of the car, my phone bleeps.

Are you close?

It's from Eve, the third of its kind since I passed Ojai on the highway.

Five minutes, I text back.

It's a few degrees cooler here than in LA and has a still quality, no hum of traffic, no sirens. I actually hear birds in the trees. It makes me feel spooked and lost. New York was too much. It drained my senses and shattered my nerves. But already I miss the chaos of Los Angeles.

When I approach the wooden Victorian structure that is Eve's sober house, a neglected building with peeling yellow paint and half-dead shrubbery on the walkway, Eve is already coming out of it. For a moment, I don't recognize the petite woman coming down the sagging steps. Then it hits me that this is Eve.

It isn't that she looks much different. The same figure exactly, small and delicately proportioned. But her face is weathered by sun and time and she has stopped coloring her hair so that it has returned to an ash blond. And I was looking for the girl I last saw sixteen years ago. She barely looks at me, and then giggles uncomfortably as we hug.

"You look the same!" I say.

"Let's go," Eve says, already leading the way.

She is walking quickly so that I have to hurry to keep up.

"Sorry," she says, when we are almost up the street. "I just needed to get *out* of there."

I want to sit still so we can talk.

"Have you had lunch?" I ask.

"What?" Eve whirls around. "No. Are you hungry? I guess I could eat."

I point to a Mexican restaurant on the corner of State Street. It has seating on the patio. "How about there?"

"Yeah," says Eve. "Okay."

She says it wearily, as if it was inevitable that we would always end up there, at that Mexican restaurant.

We're taken immediately to a table outside, where the waiter fills our glasses with ice water. He is young and Hispanic.

Finally, seated across from each other, we look at each other and smile, then laugh with embarrassment. I can't help but feel we're laughing at the fact that we've aged, just as everyone always promised we would.

"You look good," I say.

Eve waves her hand. "Whatever."

The waiter comes back with menus and I order a cup of coffee.

"I really want a glass of wine," says Eve.

I gasp. "No, Eve."

"Look, I don't have a drinking problem."

"Please don't."

She sighs. She looks at the boy who has been watching us from under his black bangs, his head ducked shyly.

"I'll take a Coke," she tells him. "A Diet Coke."

I have tortilla soup and Eve picks at a plate of chips and guacamole. She tells me how she hates the sober house, sharing a room with two girls half her age, one who has night terrors.

"I don't have a drinking problem," she says again.

I know this is not true. We used to drink together. That was half our bond.

"Why did you come here?" I ask. "Was it an intervention or something?"

"What? No. My sister said if she is going to keep giving me money, I have to come here."

I remember the sister, the one also in *Vogue*. I only met her once. She was not beautiful like Eve, only very pretty. It was why *Vogue* put her in profile. She was a year younger, and much more ambitious. Eve tells me now that her sister has been married to an investment banker for twelve years.

"I hate him," she says. "Did you ever meet him? Robert Keep?"

I shake my head. Eve always had a tendency to think everyone knew everyone else. Partially, because she herself knew most of social Manhattan. Now that I've gotten used to the changes in her face, I no longer see them. I only see the same even features, the wide eyes and high cheekbones, the bow-shaped mouth. She is young again to me.

"He's so awful," says Eve. "This is all his fault."

"What do you mean?"

She clutches at the neck of her sundress and makes an impatient gesture. "He's convinced my sister that there's something wrong with me. Do you know, he asked me out first? We went out on a date before he ever knew Leah. But now he hates me. I don't know why. He's spreading all these lies about me."

"Like what?"

"Don't you ever go on Facebook? I've put up tons of posts about it. He had a doctor say I was *schizophrenic*."

"What do you mean?"

"Leah said I had to see a psychiatrist if I wanted any financial help. And Robert sent me to his shrink who diagnosed me as schizophrenic. Can you believe it? And now he's spread it. Robert, I mean. And people in New York believe it."

"I'm sure they don't."

"I mean, no one's told me to my face. But people are treating me differently. I can feel the energy of it. Even old friends. I'm sure it's why I lost my job."

"What was your job?"

"I was working at an art gallery in Brooklyn, for this lady Rebecca Nettles. She said I was messing up the paperwork and was rude to customers. I have *never* been rude to customers."

Her eyes fill with tears of frustration. I reach over and put my hand on her forearm. She shakes her head, impatient, so I remove my hand.

"So, what about you? What are you doing these days?" she asks.

"I'm a makeup artist."

She blinks and her face lights up. Her eyes still glisten with tears, but she looks happy now.

"Oh, how amazing. Do you like it?"

"You taught me how to put on makeup. Do you remember?"

"Did I?" She smiles.

"Yes."

"No kidding."

"You were always a pro," I say.

"So do you work on movie sets?"

"Oh, no. Just events. But I have a pretty good client list. Do you ever watch any reality TV?"

Her face darkens. "It's just been a nightmare," she says. "A total nightmare. I don't belong here. I don't know what I'm even doing here."

"Maybe it's a good idea to cut out the drinking."

"I don't have a problem with wine," she says.

I laugh. "That's very specific."

She laughs, too.

"Just give it a try," I say.

She looks at me steadily. "Why did we ever lose touch?"

*   *   *

Later we walk down State Street. She decides she's hungry as we pass a Starbucks, and eats a hardboiled egg from their protein pack. I suspect she still keeps obsessive control of her figure. She eats it standing up and then stuffs the plastic container into the narrow bin.

"I started smoking again," she says when we step back outside.

"You quit?"

"For a long time. Years. But this is so stressful. It's so stressful at that place. They make us turn the lights out at ten p.m., as if we're children. This is only the second weekend I've been allowed out on my own."

As we walk down State Street, she tells me more about her brother-in-law, how he never forgave her for rejecting him, how he has spread the schizophrenic story.

"I think at our age, it's very unlikely we will develop schizophrenia," I say. "Doesn't it usually happen when you're young?"

Eve flinches.

"I mean, in your late teens and early twenties?" I say quickly.

"I don't know," she says.

"He could have come up with something better. You'd think alcoholism was enough."

She turns to me, her eyes flashing. "And *that's* not even true!"

The street is crowded with people. It's a Saturday. People mill in and out of T-shirt shops and boutiques. Homeless people, young and old, take up benches. The young ones look as if they're only playing a role, their skin smooth, their hair thick. They have nose rings and complicated tattoos and wear hooded sweatshirts, even on this hot day. Next to them their older counterparts sit hunched with empty eyes and nervous tics. One shouts at us. He points at Eve and says, "Hey, you!"

She turns and gives him a challenging look and then shakes her head. She is walking quickly again. We reach the sunbaked bridge that crosses the highway and make our way over it and down to the beach. In the distance, the long pier is festooned with flags. Eve chooses the beach to the left of it as if she has done this a hundred times, no hesitation. It is emptier of people on this side. She finally comes to a stop partway down the beach, but not very close to the water.

The ocean is full of boats, mostly sailboats. The water is jagged with the white crests of waves, the sun glinting off them. It's disorienting to be in this bright setting with her. I've only known her against a dim urban backdrop, rain-drenched avenues echoing with sirens, the artificial light of restaurants and clubs and lobbies. All this natural light and color makes her seem to me like an actress who has wandered onto the wrong soundstage.

When we sit down in the sand, she pulls out a cigarette and lights it.

"I totally lost touch with you when you moved to California," she says.

"Yes, that was a weird time."

"But you said we had a fight?"

"Well, I think. Sort of."

"What about?"

"God knows."

"It can't have been over a guy," she says. "We never dated the same type, did we? You had strange taste. You always went for these really . . . " She laughs.

"Really what?" I laugh.

"Oh, you know. Just undesirables. There was that one guy with the beard. Remember?"

"Oh, him," I say, wincing at the memory.

I think of the night I was on a date with a clean-cut type. He worked on Wall Street. When we ran into Eve in a bar on Lexington, he moved in on her.

"There was that one guy, the broker," she says, almost as if reading my mind. "What was his name? Whatever happened to him?"

"He liked you."

"Did he?"

Her wonder is genuine. Men hitting on her was just background noise to her, like traffic, a fact of life.

"That night was the last time I ever saw him," I say.

Suddenly she gets agitated. "Men just want young women. I know they think I'm past it. I can almost feel them saying *old* when they pass me. It's so rude. Men are horrible."

She carries on about this for a while, waving her cigarette around. She takes a long brooding drag off of it and digs her feet into the sand, staring at her toes. Her nail polish is a chipped blue. She pulls again at the neck of her thin cotton dress, as if it is choking her. I notice that in spite of everything, she still knows how to wear clothes. Her dress has a gossamer hippie quality, but she has worn a thick leather belt with it, something I would never think to wear. She used to try to teach me about clothes. She would wear platform heels and tell me I needed to get out of old lady shoes.

"It's so hard to get up in the morning," she says suddenly.

A terrier bounds from nowhere onto her lap and then carries on down the beach. It seems to belong to no one, a crazy black blur against the sand. An older woman in a red and gold kaftan appears from behind us and follows in its direction. Eventually, the dog circles back to her.

"You might be depressed, Eve. Have they mentioned antidepressants to you?"

This spurs another tirade about medication. She says she won't take it.

"If they want me to be sober, why do they want me to take pills that make me feel out of it?"

"What kind of pills?" I ask.

She sits up and fixes me with her green eyes. "Did my brother-in-law send you?"

"What?" I say. "No."

"He did, didn't he? Robert sent you!"

"Eve," I say, putting out a placating hand. "Robert didn't send me."

"He sent that guy back there!"

"What guy?"

"You *heard* him. That guy who yelled at me back there. The man pretending to be homeless. Robert sent him."

I take a deep breath and turn around to look at the two or three people down toward the water's edge, a middle-aged woman and two younger ones. The younger women are in shorts, the older woman in jeans. They are taking photos of one another with a phone. After each shot, they huddle around to look at it.

"Why are you looking at those people?" Eve asks. "Do you know them?"

"Hey," I say. "Let's go back."

"Back where?"

"Let's take a walk along State Street."

"We just came from there. Why do you want me to go back there? What are you trying to do?"

I feel trapped. I stand up, my knees like jelly. I realize I can't just leave her here on the beach.

To my relief, she gets up too. She has a terrible expression on her face, of anger and contempt, but she picks up her sandals and seems prepared to follow me.

"Do you want to have a coffee or something?" I ask.

"You drink so much coffee," she says mildly. "Is that what I have to do now? Just drink tons of coffee and never have a glass of wine again?"

"Ha!" I say. I start back toward the pier.

"*What are you looking at?*" she yells behind me. I turn to see her standing and facing the women at the shore. She brandishes her sandals at them.

They stand frozen, as in a tableau, the phone still the center point between them. Their expressions are a mixture of fright and wonder. They glance at me. I touch my fingers to my temple quickly and they look away, back at the phone. But Eve is still yelling at them.

*   *   *

I came up here to apologize to Eve. We never had a big fight, but we should have. Or rather, she should have fought with me. I was the reason the tide turned against her. This is what I had always thought, but now I see that the tide would have eventually turned anyway. The day after the broker tried to leave me at the bar to go off with Eve, I was at work. The wife of a gossip columnist called the office. She wanted an outfit delivered that afternoon for a gala on the weekend.

"Is Frances bringing it?" she asked.

"I am," I told her. "I'm her assistant."

The woman's apartment was in Murray Hill, with deep white carpets and Chinese screens. She had white orchids and glossy coffee-table books and malachite eggs in the room where I was told to wait for her. When she emerged, harried, her hair in a ponytail, she looked too young to be married to the columnist. I had met him once with Eve, at a party she had taken me to. Eve's face, when she talked to him, was lit with worship. He seemed so old to me, but now I suppose he was only in his early forties, my age now.

"Where's Frances?" the woman had asked, already forgetting what I had told her on the phone.

"She said to call her if there were any problems."

She sighed and took the garment bag from me. "Wait here."

She turned to me when she was almost out of the room, her expression transformed by sudden conscience, and said, "Do you want something to drink?"

"No," I said. "Thank you."

Eve had slept with her husband. He was really the only man Eve seemed to care about, so that the other men, including my broker, were like birds that knocked themselves out flying into windows when they tried to get at her. As I sat in the living room, waiting for the woman to come out in the dress, I thought of how I would bring up Eve's name.

"Can you come in here a minute?" she called.

I found her in the bedroom at the end of a long hall. She was frowning at herself in a full-length mirror, pulling at the ruched waist of an emerald-green dress. Her fingers fluttered nervously over the bodice and then she let out a deep sigh of dissatisfaction.

"It needs to be taken in a little more here and here," she said. "I'll need Frances to get it done by tomorrow."

She continued to stare at her image and for a moment her eyes drifted to her face and stopped there.

When I saw the *Vogue* sitting on the bedside table, I knew how I was going to bring up Eve's name.

* * *

I lost my job, of course. There were plenty of reasons to fire me, my lateness, my vagueness, my own dress sense, so that when I was told I was no longer needed, I did not get angry or demand answers. Frances promised me a good reference.

I expected Eve to come at me like a fury. I stopped returning her calls. Her voice was calm in her messages at first, but eventually she sounded hurt and then angry.

"Why aren't you calling me back?" she demanded. "Have I done something wrong?"

I never told her I was moving to California. By then, enough time had passed so that when I saw her at a party downtown, two weeks before I left, I found her drunk and forgiving.

"Why do you never call me back? I miss you," she said sweetly. Always sweet in her drunkenness.

That was the last time I had seen her until now, when we are walking up State Street. I brace myself to pass the small group of homeless people, who are still sharing two benches in front of a coffee shop. I pray the man doesn't say anything to Eve.

Instead, when we are almost abreast of him, she shouts, "Hey, *you!*"

The man looks up. The others around him look up, too. He is the oldest and the dirtiest, with pale eyes and a brick-red face.

"I know who sent you!" she says.

"Eve," I say, reaching for her arm. She shrugs me off.

The homeless man is shouting back at her now. He's calling her a crazy bitch. This seems to make her thoughtful. She carries on walking and I follow her.

When we are past him, she says, "See? Did you hear what he called me? He said I was crazy. That's all Robert."

When we reach the corner, she turns to me with a hard expression. "Did he send you?"

"No, Eve," I say. "I've never met Robert. I've only ever met your sister once."

She's more subdued now. We've reached a quieter section of State Street. We cross to an old theatre, the marquis advertising the *The African Queen* as part of its classic film series. She has slowed her pace so that I no longer have to hurry to keep up.

When we reach her street, I say, for lack of anything else, "It's amazing to see you after all this time."

She turns to me with wondering eyes. "So we had a fight?"

I can't lie to her now.

"Not a fight," I say.

"What, then? Was it because you moved to California?"

"I don't know. I had a lot of problems."

"That guy," she said.

"Which guy?"

"Didn't you have trouble with some guy?"

I want to confess what I did now. It's partially why I came up to see her. I've been bracing myself for it all week. The lameness of doing it sixteen years later is not lost on me, but this would have been exactly the right moment to do it, if I were to do it. If she were sane.

"Always trouble with some guy," I say.

We are near now to her sober house, but she wants to go an extra block to the park and sit.

"I really need to get going," I lie. "I need to be back in LA by four-thirty." My voice is a little shrill.

"You have to go already?" she says sadly.

I hesitate. "Well, let me think. I guess I could go for a little bit. An extra fifteen minutes."

When we get to the park, she takes out her pack of cigarettes again. It makes me realize I did not see her put out her last cigarette. Maybe she left it burning in the sand. We are sitting in a soft shaded area under a jacaranda tree. It's a small park, only really a square of land with a path cutting through it. She toys with the pack of cigarettes, and I examine her face up close. Except for her skin, which is coarse now, I decide that she is exactly the same. Nothing about her has changed.

She puts the cigarette pack down and says, "I know what you're going to tell me."

For a moment, my heart is in my throat. "Oh?"

She rolls her eyes. "That I'm still pretty. It's what everyone tells me. I know they're just saying it."

"But you are," I say, able to breathe again.

"I'm sick of everyone lying to me. Everyone making excuses about why they can't see me. It's because of these *pernicious* rumors that Robert started. That I'm crazy."

I am concentrating on the grass now, which looks a little patchy, affected by the drought.

"Do you really have to go so soon?" she asks.

I look at my watch. She is calmer now, so I say, "Maybe not right away."

"I'm sorry, Kate."

"For what?"

She waves her hand, indicating State Street, the homeless man. For a moment she is back, and it's as if she's apologizing for someone else, a third person along with us.

"Oh, that's okay," I say.

"It's just so hard when you know people are spreading lies about you."

Something rustles in the tree overhead, a bird or a squirrel, making the shadows ripple over her face. For a moment I am stunned to find myself here with her, in this peaceful park, as if we are in another life altogether.

"I can imagine," I say. "It must be terrible."

LAURA DEMERS was born in New York, NY. She received an MA in English Education from New York University and an MA in Creative and Life Writing from Goldsmiths College in London. Her first short story was published in the North American Review *and she was nominated in 2017 for the PEN/Robert J. Dau Short Story Prize for Emerging Writers. She currently lives in Los Angeles.*

CPSIA information can be obtained
at www.ICGtesting.com
Printed in the USA
LVHW05s1708290918
591788LV00004B/7/P